Behind Closed Doors

The lock clicked and the door opened a crack. One eye looked at her for a moment, then Henry opened the door wide. "Quick," he said. "I don't want anybody to see us."

She slipped through and he locked the door behind her.

He reached for the portfolio and she placed it in his hand. The intensity of the relief on his face as he glanced inside was almost embarrassing to see. His intensity both disturbed and attracted her. It was as if she had unknowingly broken something important to him and now he was expecting her to make it whole again.

"I'd better go now," Janie said. "Would you mind unlocking the door?"

Books from Scholastic
in the **Couples** series:

#1 *Change of Hearts*
#2 *Fire and Ice*
#3 *Alone, Together*
#4 *Made for Each Other*
#5 *Moving Too Fast*
#6 *Crazy Love*
#7 *Sworn Enemies*
#8 *Making Promises*
#9 *Broken Hearts*
#10 *Secrets*
#11 *More Than Friends*
#12 *Bad Love*
#13 *Changing Partners*
#14 *Picture Perfect*
#15 *Coming on Strong*

Couples Special Edition
    Summer Heat!

Coming Soon ...

#16 *Sweethearts*
#17 *Dance With Me*

MADE FOR EACH OTHER

By M.E. Cooper

SCHOLASTIC INC.
New York Toronto London Auckland Sydney

ISBN 0-590-33393-3

12 11 10 9 8 7 6 5 4 3   6 7 8 9/8 0/9

Printed in the U.S.A.   06

MADE FOR EACH OTHER

Chapter
1

Janie Barstow walked down the hall with her eyes fixed on the floor in front of her. An entire day had passed without any disasters. Maybe this semester was going to be better than the last. It could hardly be much worse.

"Hi there."

She glanced over. Barry, a guy she knew from history class, had come up alongside her. "Hi," she said.

"How was your Christmas vacation?"

"Great." In reality, it had been boring at best. She was invited to two parties, and left both of them early.

Barry was still there, matching her step for step. She had to say something. "How was yours?" she asked.

He beamed. "Terrific. Really terrific. I went on a learn-to-ski week. The weather was great, the parties were great, and the other kids were

1

great, too. And skiing is really terrific fun. How about you, do you ski?"

"Not really."

"You ought to learn," he said. "It's really easy, the way they teach it. You start out with short skis and then as you get better you switch to longer ones, until you're up to regular size. By Saturday I was going down most of the trails on the mountain. Hey, didn't I see you hanging around the school radio station? Do you work there or something?"

Beneath her long, floppy bangs, Janie's face turned bright red. Volunteering for the radio station had been her mother's idea. At first Janie had loved it — and loved Kennedy High's radio celebrity, disc jockey Peter Lacey. That wasn't unusual. Half the girls at Kennedy seemed to have a crush on Peter. He never seemed to notice.

After helping him with his show day after day, Janie had started to think that he was as interested in her as she was in him. When he casually asked her to help him with the records at the annual homecoming dance, she managed to convince herself that he was really asking her for a date. She discovered the embarrassing truth — that he was in love with skater Lisa Chang and wanted to take *her* — only at the last minute.

Peter and Lisa did everything they could to make Janie feel comfortable. They even arranged for Brad Davidson, the student body president, to take her to the dance. She managed to enjoy the evening. But she quit the radio station after the incident, and since then she avoided Peter whenever she could.

"Er . . . not anymore," she finally said to Barry. "It didn't leave me enough time to study."

"Oh. Too bad. I was thinking maybe you could get a free learn-to-ski trip if you told them you wanted to do a radio show about it. Did you ever do anything like that?"

"No."

"Really? I bet people do it all the time, though. Take Peter Lacey. He must go to all the concerts and clubs and have a super record collection, all freebies."

"He does not!" Jane stopped in the middle of the hallway and turned to glare at Barry. "Every record that comes in is the property of the station. Peter has never taken one of them for himself. He even buys records with his own money, if there's something the station doesn't have that he thinks it needs."

"Hey, okay!" Barry held up his hands in mock surrender. "I don't know the guy, and besides, I think he does a terrific show."

Janie's shyness returned double-strength. Why had she blown up like that? Peter Lacey didn't need her to defend him. Besides, he probably did get into clubs and concerts free sometimes. The way he kept on the lookout for hot new groups to promote, he deserved to.

"That's all right," she mumbled. Her outburst must have told Barry much more about her feelings for Peter than she wanted anyone to know. She glanced at him again. He looked bored and restless.

Sure enough, his next words were, "Well, hey, see you in class, right?"

3

"Right."

He turned down a short hall that led to the quad and vanished. Janie suppressed a sigh. Why couldn't she carry on a nice, normal conversation without either disappearing into the wallpaper, or blowing up like a firecracker left over from the Fourth of July?

In Cincinnati, Janie had had real friends, friends she had known for years. Friends who didn't care when she suddenly became the tallest kid in class. Friends who didn't call her names like Beanpole and Olive Oyl. But last year when her folks made the move to Rose Hill, a suburb of Washington, D.C., everything changed. The ways the other kids spent their time, the way they dressed, the way they talked — all of it was different from what she was used to.

It wouldn't have been so bad if she had the looks and personality to make herself popular. Laurie Bennington had moved to Rose Hill a year before, too, but what a difference! Laurie had a beautiful face, a great figure, and the clothes to show them off. She also had the kind of brash self-confidence that let her throw a big party right after she moved to town and still didn't know anybody. She had invited everybody who counted at Kennedy High, and most of them showed up. Laurie quickly became one of the people who counted, with a student government post and her own regular spot on Peter Lacey's radio show.

But Janie was not Laurie. She was about as far from being Laurie as it was possible to get, with her long brown hair, straight figure, and uninteresting face. She could never be glib and witty the way Laurie was, either. And she was *still* taller than practically all of the girls and a lot of the boys in her class!

As she neared a turn in the hallway, she heard a sound that made her freeze. Everybody at Kennedy knew that laugh and that voice. She took a cautious peek. Sure enough, there was Peter Lacey, standing twenty feet away in the middle of the hallway, talking to someone. His back was to her, but he was wearing his familiar brown leather bomber jacket and carrying a stack of records under one arm. Her heartbeat quickened at the sight of him. Not that she still had romantic dreams about him; she had awakened from those weeks ago. But seeing him reminded her of how foolish she had been to have such dreams at all.

Peter started to turn around. She ducked back, but not before she had seen that he was talking to Sasha Jenkins. Sasha was a kind, friendly girl, one of the nicest people in the junior class, but she was also one of the last people Janie wanted to see just then.

Sasha was a reporter and editor for the Kennedy newspaper. After Janie left the radio station, her mom urged her to volunteer for another extracurricular activity. Finally, just to get her mom to let her alone, she had decided to help with the newspaper. One reason was that she'd be working for Sasha. That seemed a lot less emotionally complicated than being constantly around some other Peter Lacey. But the first thing Sasha asked her to do was to take copies of the new issue around to the paper's advertisers in Georgetown.

Janie's cheeks burned as she recalled that afternoon. At the first couple of places she went to, the people smiled, and said thanks when she gave them their papers. But then she had to take the paper to Rezato. Rezato was one of the fanciest boutiques in Washington, the sort of place with such chic clothes in the window that you couldn't imagine seeing anyone actually *wearing* them. When Janie handed her the newspaper, the Rezato manager discovered that the shop's full-page ad had somehow been printed as a quarter-page. Janie was the only available target for her fury, and she delivered it full blast. On the bus home she made up her mind to have nothing more to do with the school paper. Janie Barstow simply didn't have the brash enthusiasm of Sasha Jenkins, and she never would.

Around the corner, Sasha's and Peter's voices were getting louder. Janie was sure she could hear footsteps, too. She *couldn't* face Peter, not yet, and if Sasha saw her, she'd probably ask her to deliver papers again. Frantically she looked around. The nearest cross corridor was too far; she'd never get there in time.

Her only escape was to duck into a classroom. The first two doors led to a boiler room and a janitor's closet, both locked, of course. The next was the home ec room. That was sure to be locked as well; it was full of sewing machines, cooking utensils, and other equipment. But as she passed the door, she gave the knob a hopeless twist. To her surprise and relief, it turned. She instantly

6

opened the door a crack, slipped through, and closed the door, just as Sasha's approaching voice said, "People sure clear out fast after school, don't they?"

Janie closed her eyes, took a deep breath, and let it out in a sigh. That had been a close call. Suddenly she stiffened at a rustling sound somewhere in the room. Someone else was there with her.

Janie tried to keep her body relaxed, but she left one hand on the knob just in case she decided to fling the door open and run. Then she opened her eyes just a crack and peeked around the room. On the far side, near the windows, someone was standing, staring at her — a tall, slim boy with blond hair that flopped down over his eyes. After a moment, she remembered him. His name was Henry Braverman. They had shared an art class the previous spring, her first semester at Kennedy. She remembered him for two reasons: His name was right after hers in roll call every morning, and he was one of the few students in the class who was taller than she was. He looked almost as startled by her entrance as she felt at finding him in the room.

"Oh, hi," she said, twisting the hem of her jacket between nervous fingers. "I'm sorry I disturbed you. I didn't know there was anybody in here."

Instead of answering, he turned his back on her and started shoveling what looked like a bunch of cloth scraps into a big manila envelope.

"That's okay," he replied abruptly. "It's time for me to go anyway."

7

He crossed the room, stopped a couple of feet away, and looked at her again. She thought he was about to say something more, but he tucked the manila envelope under one arm and jammed both fists into his coat pockets. Janie suddenly realized that she was blocking the door. Her face burning, she stepped aside and said, "Sorry."

He said something in return as he left the room, but what it was she couldn't tell. Then the door hissed closed and she was alone in the room. She knew that she should leave, too, but she imagined walking out and bumping into Peter and Sasha, still standing there talking. They were probably long since gone, but it wouldn't hurt her to wait a few more minutes just in case.

As Janie waited, she wondered why Henry Braverman had been in the home ec room after school. His face had guilt written all over it. He must have been doing something he shouldn't have been.

A noise out in the hall made her stomach somersault. She had to leave before someone else came into the room and asked for an explanation. As she turned to go, her foot knocked into a large, flat, zippered case leaning against the wall. Startled, she caught it as it began to topple. Without thinking, she carried it into the corridor before looking at it more closely. On an adhesive label in one corner was written: "Henry Braverman, 132 Winding Way, Rose Hill, MD." The lettering was tall, spiky, and very elegant.

Her first impulse was to return it to the home ec room. Henry might come back to look for it and be upset if it wasn't there. But now that she was out of the room, she didn't know if she could force herself to go back in. Besides, it was really her fault that he had left in such a rush and forgotten it. She knew where Winding Way was, not very far from her own house. In fact, it was more or less on her way home. She would take the portfolio to Henry as a kind of apology for disturbing him, whatever he had been doing.

As she walked through the quiet suburban streets, Janie imagined that she was in the opening chapter of one of the fantasy novels she loved to read. At some moment when she least expected it, a door would open and she would step into a different world. There she would face deadly perils of every sort, but her intelligence and courage would carry her through. In the end she would save the people of the endangered city where she found herself, and be hailed as priestess and queen. There would be a king, of course. For a long time he had borne a peculiar resemblance to Peter Lacey, but this afternoon she noticed that his features had become much hazier. He did seem to be growing thinner, though, and taller.

Janie was summoned back to Rose Hill by the toot of a car horn. She took a hasty step back onto the curb to let a bright red Camaro turn in front of her. Looking around, she realized she had reached Winding Way.

Winding Way had been named by someone whose imagination was even more active than hers. It was as straight as any street in town. The houses on either side were a little smaller than Janie's. Most of them had tricycles or bicycles in the front yard and basketball hoops mounted over the garage. When she got to 132, she found the red Camaro sitting in the driveway. A decal boosting the Wildcats, Rose Hill State College's football team, decorated its rear window. As she was trying to decide what to do, a man came out of the garage with a chamois cloth in his hand. He wasn't unusually tall, but his broad shoulders and beefy arms made him seem huge. He was a little younger than Janie's father, with crew-cut blond hair that was starting to turn gray.

He noticed her. Before she could turn away, he called, "Looking for someone, miss?"

"Is this —" she began, too softly for him to hear. Swallowing hard, she walked up the driveway and tried again. "Is this where Henry Braverman lives?"

He tossed the chamois on the car hood, stuck his enormous hands in the pockets of his blue running suit, and said, "I'm Henry Braverman. What can I do for you?"

She blinked in confusion. This man couldn't be Henry's father. She didn't see any resemblance. "Ah —"

"I know," he said with a chuckle. "You must want Hank. Henry junior," he added when her expression remained baffled. "My son. Are you a friend of his from school?"

"Er. . . ."

"I'm afraid he's not home yet. He stays late for basketball practice every day, you know. You've seen him play, haven't you?"

"Well, I don't. . . ." Janie began.

"You ought to," he continued, without listen-

10

ing. "It means a lot to a team to know that their schoolmates are behind them a hundred percent."

"I've got to go," she mumbled, ducking her head to avoid his intense gaze.

"I'll tell Hank you came by. Being so active in athletics doesn't leave him time for much of a social life, but he'll be sorry he missed you. Any message you want me to give him?"

"No. No thanks. I. . . ." Flapping her hand helplessly, she turned and walked away very quickly.

"Hey! Miss! What's your name?"

She pretended not to hear and kept walking. Something about the man had made her feel twice as shy as usual, and her puzzlement only added to her desire to get away. Henry hadn't been at basketball practice that afternoon; he'd been lurking in the home ec room. But she hadn't felt like mentioning that to his father. Not that he had given her much of a chance to mention anything.

As she was walking up her driveway, she realized that she still had Henry's portfolio with her. As she entered the house through the kitchen door, she paused to listen for activity, then escaped to her favorite lair in the basement. It was pretty dusty, and one corner was cluttered with all her mom's sewing equipment; but the couch was comfortable, the lamp was bright, and her bookcase was jammed with all her favorite science fiction and fantasy novels. Best of all, Betty and Beverly, her ten-year-old twin sisters, didn't bug her down there.

She unwound the muffler from her neck, tossed

her brown wool coat on the back of the couch, and placed the portfolio carefully on the battered old desk. Fingering the zipper pull, she looked down at the case for a long time. Finally she tucked her hair back behind her ears, brushed her hands off on her beige corduroy jumper, and unzipped it.

She could see that it held a thin stack of papers. She reached in, then pulled her hand back. She would hate it if anyone rummaged through her private papers. But her encounters with Henry and his father had left her unbearably curious.

Holding her breath, she reached in again and pulled out the sheaf.

"Oh!" Janie gasped. The top page was a sketch of a tall, lean, angular girl with hair cut short on one side and falling over her eye on the other. She was wearing a lacy blouse and a pale green skirt with a hemline that dipped low in front and back, and rose to knee height on either side. Stapled to the top of the page was a small square of pale green patterned fabric.

Janie leafed carefully through the rest of the pages. Each one portrayed a different outfit on a different model. There were sports dresses and jumpers, caftans and raincapes, even a long formal gown. Many of them, like the first, had small swatches of fabric attached. Each was as striking and different as the first one, and each was signed at the bottom, in a spiky, elegant hand: *Henry Braverman.*

Chapter
2

"Okay, Cardinals, it's lunchtime once again, and time to rock. Let's give a good listen to some new sounds from a driving Detroit band called the Four-Speed Box!" A thumping bass line, punctuated by rim shot triplets from the drums, filled the cafeteria. Peter Lacey was on the air again, doing his daily show on WKND, the school radio station. Sasha smiled as she carried her tray to one of the tables in the north corner, where the crowd ate when it was too cold to use the quad. She knew why so many people liked Peter's show: He obviously had fun doing it.

As Sasha put her tray down, she noticed Laurie Bennington sauntering toward her with a purposeful look on her face. Heads turned as Laurie passed. She was wearing a pair of shiny black pants and an oversized gray cable-knit sweater that matched her soft gray suede elf boots. The only touches of color were provided by two green silk scarves, one holding her lustrous black hair and the other knotted at the hips, just tightly enough to emphasize her figure. Sasha didn't envy Laurie's fashion sense, it was too different from her own taste, but she certainly admired it. Laurie was a knockout.

"Sasha, how *are* you?" Laurie said in an emotion-filled voice. She sounded as if the two were lifelong friends just meeting again after years apart.

"Okay," Sasha said. She lifted the top of her yogurt container and sprinkled on the nuts, grains, and dried fruits she had brought from home. As she stirred, she added, "How about you? Did you have a nice holiday?"

"So-so. My parents insisted on taking me to Curacao, in the West Indies. The beach was utterly empty and went on forever, but everyone there was about a hundred and fifty years old. I got so bored that I finally sneaked out one night, and went to a disco with the boy who took care of the beach umbrellas." She heaved a sigh and adjusted the neckline of her sweater to let a shapely, well-tanned shoulder show. "That's why I haven't had a chance till now to tell you how much I loved your article on all those old rituals. It was simply *thrilling.*"

Just before the holidays, Sasha had published an essay in the school paper about the customs of ancient midwinter festivals and how they survived in the celebrations of Christmas and New Year's Day. She had really enjoyed doing the research and writing it up, but Laurie was the first person to mention it to her. She flushed with pleasure and

14

said, "Thanks, I'm glad you liked it."

"Liked it? Of course I did! Why, the first thing I do every week when I pick up *The Red and the Gold* is look for your byline. I hope I won't offend you by saying this, but I think you're the only real journalist the paper has."

Instead of responding, Sasha started eating her yogurt. It may have been disloyal of her to listen to Laurie's compliments, but it certainly was nice to be appreciated. Too many of the kids seemed to think that the paper just appeared magically every week. They didn't realize how much hard work went into it.

Perhaps Laurie had decided to turn over a new leaf. Sasha knew Laurie had done some unkind things in the past. Peter had told her the whole story of how Laurie had tricked Janie into believing he cared about her, just to embarrass Peter. But Sasha also believed that everyone had a positive side — even Laurie, if she would let it show.

"It's a shame the paper isn't central to the life of the school," Laurie continued. "Instead of reading, everybody just listens to *that*."

She motioned toward the loudspeaker in the ceiling. As the last notes of a song faded, Peter said, "The latest and best, a side that will last, and you heard it first right here on WKND where the tunes keep spinnin' and I keep grinnin'." The opening notes of Bruce Springsteen's latest hit came up from under his rap.

"I think Peter's great," Sasha said. "He knows how to keep people listening."

"Oh, so do I," Laurie said hastily. "Peter and I are great friends. But wouldn't it be nice if *The*

15

Red and the Gold got the same kind of recognition and support from students that the radio station does? It certainly deserves it. Why, *you* should be as famous at Kennedy as Peter is, maybe even more famous. He just talks and plays records, after all. That doesn't take the kind of thought and research that goes into one of your articles, does it?"

"I don't know, I've never done a radio show. You do one, don't you?"

Laurie gave a high, tinkly laugh. "I did for a while. You probably know that I'm the student activities officer for student council."

Sasha nodded, though she wasn't at all sure what the job of a student activities officer was.

"I thought I could help get students more involved," Laurie continued, "by making sure everyone knew what was happening around here. I guess it worked too well. There are some people who don't want more real involvement. They want to keep everything in the hands of a small clique, just the way it's always been. That's why my show was taken off the air."

"But that's awful," Sasha exclaimed. "Who are these people you're talking about? That's just the kind of story we should be printing in *The Red and the Gold*."

Laurie's eyes shifted nervously from side to side. "No, no," she said quickly, "what I told you is strictly off the record. I don't want to get you into trouble, too."

Laurie looked over Sasha's shoulder and her expression hardened. Sasha glanced backward. "Oh, hi, Chris. Hi, Ted. Join us."

16

Sasha thought Chris Austin and Ted Mason were the most attractive couple she knew. Ted had broad shoulders, narrow hips, and a slow, easy smile as casual as the jeans and pullovers he usually wore. He was the school's star quarterback, and Chris was a top student and head of the honor society. She was also, as of a couple of months before, the junior class homecoming princess. That had been a tribute to her school spirit as much as to her all-American blond beauty.

Ted glanced at Chris before saying, "Sure."

As they pulled out chairs, Laurie stood up and said, "Sorry to rush off, but I have a lot to do. I'll drop by the journalism room later, Sasha. There are some ideas I'd like to share with you about the paper." She nodded to Ted, ignored Chris, and walked away, leaving her tray on the table.

"Brrr," Ted said with a grin.

"What was she doing here, Sasha?" Chris asked grimly.

"Talking to me about the newspaper."

Ted was still grinning. "Uh-oh, watch out!"

"What for? Why are you so down on her?"

"Look, Sash," Chris said, "it's true that I still resent the things Laurie said over the radio during her campaign to keep me off the Homecoming Court — not just about me, but about Brenda, too." Brenda, Chris's stepsister, was just starting to live down the bad reputation she had made in her first months at Kennedy High. "But I'll be as objective as I can: Laurie Bennington is a mean, scheming, nasty, conniving —"

Ted reached over and put two fingers across her

17

lips. "Don't let her get to you, sweetheart," he said.

Chris took a deep breath and tugged at the tab collar of her Oxford-cloth shirt. "If Laurie wants to talk to you about the newspaper," she continued in a calmer tone, "it means that she wants to use you and the paper. How, or for what, I don't know, but you can be sure of that."

Sasha's deep feeling for the underdog took over. "No, I can't, Chris," she said, "and you can't either; whatever Laurie's done is in the past. Maybe she's feeling sorry for it now. Lots of people get off on the wrong foot, but make up for it later. Doesn't she deserve the same chance as anyone else?"

For a moment Chris's face became very stern, then she relaxed and patted Sasha's arm. "Sure she does. Maybe the leopard has changed her spots and turned into a lamb. But Sasha — when Laurie's around, keep your back to the wall. It's safer that way."

Sasha's desk in the newspaper office was even more cluttered than usual. In addition to her usual duties as a writer and editor, she was covering for Chuck Couch, the paper's business manager, who was still out with the flu. So far her efforts had produced a mixture of chaos, confusion, and disaster.

She still didn't understand how, but in the big pre-holiday issue, a full-page ad for a Washington boutique had turned into a quarter-page ad. The Roy Rogers restaurant near school, which had paid for a quarter-page, received a very impressive full-page instead. Either someone at the printer's hated designer jumpsuits and loved roast beef sandwiches, or she had made a dopey mistake when she helped prepare the issue.

However it had happened, Sasha was determined not to let it happen again. She found the stack of ad orders for the coming issue buried under a pile of photos and began sorting through them. Most of them were for one-eighth page or even smaller, from local merchants who wanted to make a gesture of support, but didn't really expect any benefit from their ads. There was also a dignified half-page from a brokerage firm. The son of one of the firm's partners was a freshman who wanted to work on the paper.

Roy Rogers had ordered another quarter-page. Sasha hoped they wouldn't be disappointed when they saw it. It wasn't going to make nearly the splash of that accidental full-page. And Rezato, the boutique, was cutting back to a quarter-page. Whatever the reason, it certainly left a hole in the paper's budget.

That left Superjock. Superjock was the paper's biggest supporter. The sporting goods store was actually taking out a two-page spread this time, in spite of the mixup over their advance copies of the previous issue. Sasha glanced at the copy for the ad. It announced a big January sale and listed some of the specials. Interested, she started reading more closely. She'd been meaning to get a new pair of running shoes for a couple of months, and she wouldn't mind saving some money on them.

She jumped as hot breath touched the nape of her neck. When she tried to get up, two beefy hands clamped her shoulders and held her in her chair. "What the —" she exclaimed.

"How's my favorite little fox?" a lazy, arrogant voice asked just behind her left ear.

"Let go of me!" She twisted her head. John Marquette's big face with its tiny eyes was only inches away.

"What'll you give me if I do?"

He slid his hands down onto her upper arms. She tried to pull away, but she knew how hopeless that was. John was a champion wrestler, as well as a starting player on the school football team. If he decided to hold onto her, there was not much she could do. A small tendril of fear touched her mind.

"Give you?" she repeated. "I'll give you more than you bargained for if you *don't* let go. Come on, John, back off! Do I have to scream for help?"

He laughed in her face. "I love it when you get mad," he said. But he did release her arms and circle around to plop himself on her desktop. She barely managed to rescue the pile of photos in time.

"So," he continued, pointing to the papers in her hand, "did I come through for my foxette or didn't I?"

She pushed her chair back to give herself a little more distance. "How many times do I have to tell you not to call me that?" she said sharply. "I am not yours, and I am not a foxette, or a little fox, or any kind of animal at all. And I don't know what you mean by coming through for me."

"Don't you? Do you think my cousin takes out two-page ads in every stupid high school paper in town? He counts on *me* for advice on getting kids into the store, and I told him to put a big ad in the Kennedy paper."

Sasha wondered how John's cousin had managed to build such a successful store if he was idiot enough to ask John for advice. But she kept her question to herself.

"He didn't like it, see," Marquette continued, reaching a hand under his sweatshirt to scratch. "He was really teed off about getting his paper late last time, especially after I'd told him my picture was going to be in it."

"I already explained —"

"Sure, sure, you explained. Big deal. He was still mad. But I told him how everybody here knows me, see, and knows I work at Superjock, so it's just good business to advertise in your little rag." He paused to give her a leer. "That was all baloney, really. I did it all for my favorite foxette."

Sasha pushed her chair back and stood up. She took a handful of papers from the desk, evading John's attempt to grab her, and headed for the door. If she couldn't get him to leave, she would leave herself. "Thanks," she said coolly. "I'm sure your cousin'll get his money's worth from his ad. Everybody at Kennedy reads *The Red and the Gold* and likes to support our advertisers. I have to go. Putting out a newspaper is a lot of work."

"Hey, what about my interview, huh? You didn't forget, did you? My cousin was real happy to hear about it and wanted to know when it would be coming out."

Sasha stopped and chewed on the inside of her cheek. She *had* promised the beefy wrestler an

21

interview before Christmas. He had threatened to tell his cousin to stop advertising in *The Red and the Gold* after the mixup over the papers. It hadn't seemed like a bad way to soothe his anger. John wasn't particularly swift upstairs; she thought she could manage to get him to spill some of the inside dirt on the athletic department. There was sure to be a terrific story there. If only getting it didn't mean spending time with John Marquette!

"Well. . . ." she said.

"Listen, sweetie, you owe me. You wouldn't have gotten that humongous ad if it wasn't for promising me that interview, see, so you'd better come through. My cousin might be real upset if I tell him you backed out after he's been bragging to his friends and customers about it."

Sasha was very tired of hearing about Marquette's cousin. It violated journalistic ethics to let an advertiser, or an advertiser's *cousin*, tell her what stories to write. It was practically the same as blackmail. She was strongly tempted to tell Marquette to shove off — and his cousin as well. On the other hand, the paper *did* need advertising money from Superjock.

"Don't worry, John," she said, "you'll get your interview."

"All right! Don't you worry either, little fox. I'll make it a night you'll never forget." He narrowed his eyes until they practically disappeared.

"Night?" Sasha backed toward the door. "What do you mean? We can do it right here in school. How's Thursday during lunch?"

"Oh, no, you don't. We're having dinner together at a place I know. That was part of the deal." He leaned against the door, one arm on either side of her, and a look of cunning took over his face. "I need to be relaxed," he continued. "You don't want an uptight interview, do you?"

After a moment's thought, she decided that he had a point. If she could get him to relax and let down his guard a little, he might let something slip that she could use. A restaurant might be the safest place of all. He couldn't move in on her in a public place.

"Okay," she said briskly, "how about a week from Friday?"

"You got it, little fox. And between now and then you can just dream about me, huh?"

Sasha shuddered. She would rather dream about a steady diet of nothing but preservatives.

Chapter
3

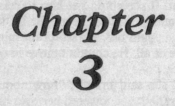

From the lunchroom came the sound of Peter's noontime show. Janie stared down at her tray and remembered what it had been like to work as his assistant. She had been proud of her skill at keeping the record library in order, finding just the cut he wanted in plenty of time, making sure he ate something and got an occasional whiff of fresh air. She had loved to watch him dancing around to the music he was sending out over the air. She had even joined in now and then. But most of all she had loved the feeling of closeness between her and Peter. She had mistaken it for romance, but looking back she saw that it was the same closeness that grows up among teammates, and people working together toward a goal. She missed it very much.

He had invited her to come back the last time they had talked. He had even offered her the post of station manager. But she couldn't accept. She knew she could never work that closely with him again. Every time she saw him, she would remember what a fool she had made of herself and know that he remembered, too. She couldn't stand that.

The girl next to her on line cleared her throat loudly. Janie looked up. The line had moved on, leaving a large gap in front of her. Beyond it, where the line curved left to the cashier's table, she saw Laurie Bennington. As usual, Laurie looked stunning, in shiny black tights and a sweater that barely reached her thighs. Janie's stomach lurched. She lowered her eyes hastily and hoped that Laurie wouldn't notice her.

Why should she feel so ashamed to run into Laurie? It wasn't fair! *Laurie* was the one who had lied and schemed and used Janie, just to get back at Peter Lacey for not falling for her. Laurie used everyone, if she could. But she strutted around as if she owned the school, while Janie, whose only mistake had been to become too fond of Peter, slunk around like a criminal.

"Hey, are you feeling all right?"

Janie looked up. The gap had become much bigger.

"Sorry," Janie muttered. She pushed her tray along. Moments later she realized that she had scooted right past the milk dispenser. By then it was too late. She couldn't go back. Her stomach gave her another twinge.

Past the cashier, she scanned the lunchroom carefully. She didn't see Henry Braverman anywhere. She had been on the lookout for him all morning, but their paths hadn't crossed. His portfolio was sitting safely in her locker, but she was determined to give it back as soon as she could. She was sure he must feel terrible, not knowing what had happened to it.

Laurie was in the corner where the in-crowd ate, talking to Sasha. She hastily turned the other way, nearly hitting someone with her tray. "Sorry," she mumbled once again.

There was an empty table in an undistinguished part of the lunchroom, far from where Laurie and Sasha were encamped. She sat down and began to pick listlessly at her chow mein. It wasn't good, but it wasn't really awful. Sometimes she felt the same way about her life. It was much more satisfying to pursue one of her fantasies.

This time she was a sorceress on a distant world. Since childhood she had been trained to focus her powers through the jewel she wore on her left index finger. Now she was standing alone on a mountaintop, gathering every wisp of cloud in the sky, and concentrating them into a thunderhead. As a breeze began to blow her diaphanous dress, she used her mental force to direct the rain cloud over a distant forest where an unnoticed fire was about to explode into a blaze. The pleated skirt of her dress billowed behind her in the wind, tugging at the pale blue satin sash. At her left shoulder, the gauzy material was slipping down onto her arm, and —

That was odd. She seemed to be paying more attention to her dress than to her adventure. Odder still, she was sure she had seen the dress somewhere before. Suddenly she realized that it was not *her* dress at all. It was one that she had been looking at the night before, in Henry's drawings.

After her last class, Janie waited by her locker until the hall emptied, then made her way to the home ec room. She kept telling herself that there was no reason to feel scared. She was doing Henry a favor by returning his drawings. Why should her heart pound so? Why did she have to fight to to catch her breath?

She considered leaning the portfolio against the door to the room, knocking, and running away. Quickly, before she had time to think any more about it, she grabbed the doorknob and twisted.

The door was locked.

Letting out the breath she had been holding, Janie turned away and started down the corridor. She was just going to have to keep looking for Henry during school. She was bound to see him in a day or two. Or she could go by his house again in the afternoon, but that might mean running into his father. She didn't want to do that.

Janie hesitated. The door's being locked didn't necessarily mean Henry wasn't there. After the way she had burst in on him yesterday, he might have decided to play it safe, and keep the door locked while he was in there. She walked back toward the room.

Janie tappend gently, then waited. Nothing happened. Taking a deep breath, she rapped hard three times. But the door remained closed.

She was turning away again when she thought

she heard a slight rustling noise inside the room. She had a sudden image of Henry standing by the door, holding his breath, and listening. The loud knocking must have startled him. He probably was expecting some teacher or one of the watchmen to discover him.

She put her head next to the door and said in a low voice, "Henry, are you in there? It's me, Janie Barstow."

No answer. "I was here yesterday," she added. But there was still no answer. She felt like a total fool, standing there in the hallway talking to a closed door. It was no use; he wasn't there. But she couldn't leave without taking one last shot. "Let me in, Henry," she said, slightly louder. "I have something of yours."

The lock clicked and the door opened a crack. One eye looked at her for a moment, then Henry opened the door wide. "Quick," he said. "I don't want anybody to see us."

She slipped through and he locked the door behind her. She looked around, but the only clue to what he was up to was a small pile of material on a table next to an old sewing machine.

She blushed as she realized that she was prying again. "Uh . . ." she said, "you left this behind yesterday. I'm sorry I broke in on you like that. I didn't know anybody was here, and there were some people out in the hall I didn't feel like seeing, so I just —"

"That's okay." He pushed his blond hair out of his eyes. "You surprised me, that's all. I didn't expect anybody to come in, and I was concentrating really hard on something, so when the door opened like that, I couldn't think what to say or do. I guess that's why I forgot my stuff."

He reached for the portfolio and she placed it in his hand. The intensity of the relief on his face as he glanced inside was almost embarrassing to see. To cover up, Janie found herself beginning to chatter.

"I'm glad I noticed it. I almost didn't, and then when I did I couldn't decide what to do about it. It didn't seem like a good idea to leave it here overnight. I could have just taken it home, I guess, but then I saw your address on the sticker. Where I live isn't very far from Winding Way, so it wasn't really any bother for me to drop it by your house. It was so confusing, though, when I asked your dad if that was where Henry Braverman lived, and he told me *he* was Henry Braverman."

"My father?" Henry said, holding himself very still. "You talked to my father?"

The way he looked and the way his voice shook frightened Janie. "I . . ." She faltered. "Not really talked to him. He was standing in the driveway, and I asked him if that was where you lived, and he — he said you were still at basketball practice."

"Oh no!" His eyes closed in pain. "What did you say? You didn't tell him you'd seen me here, did you?"

His intensity both disturbed and attracted her. It was as if she had unknowingly broken something important to him and now was expected to make it whole again. "I didn't tell him anything," she insisted. "I didn't even tell him my

29

name. I didn't know what to do, so I just went home." As Henry opened his eyes again, Janie quickly looked away.

"I'd better go now," Janie added. "Would you mind unlocking the door?"

After a moment he looked at her and said, "Huh? Oh, sure, the door." But as Henry reached for the lock he added, "Hey, listen, I'm sorry, I ought to thank you for bringing back my portfolio."

"You're welcome," Janie said stiffly.

"No, I mean it," he insisted. "It was really nice of you, and I shouldn't have let loose like that. It's just that . . . my father, he didn't see what's in here, did he?"

"Of course not! I already told you — I asked if you lived there, and then I got confused by the names and all, and walked away without saying another word."

"Oh. Right." His eyes took on that faraway look again, but after a long pause he remembered that she was there and said, "My father and I don't always get along very well."

Janie found herself starting to warm to him. There was something so vulnerable about him. He seemed like someone she could talk to without worrying that her words would end up being used against her.

"I know," she said. "It's awful when that happens, isn't it?" She turned away from him and began to trace a design on a desktop with her fingertip. "My mom's the one I have some problems with. We used to be really close, you know? But ever since we moved to Rose Hill last year, she's been pushing for me to do things that just don't feel right. It's like she doesn't even see me anymore, just someone she made up. She always says she's only thinking of what's best for me, but I wish she'd let me think for myself instead."

"That's right," he replied. "My father is always trying to make me into somebody I'm not. Or what's even worse, to *pretend* that I'm somebody I'm not."

Something gave her the courage to say, "You mean like a basketball player?"

He looked at her sharply. She wondered if she should apologize, or act as if she hadn't meant anything by her question. Instead she gave him a smile that had some slyness mixed in with its warmth. He deserved to be needled a little, after the way he had interrogated her.

He returned the smile reluctantly. "That's right."

"You're pretty tall," she said. "I bet you could make the basketball team if you wanted to."

"But I *don't* want to!" He stopped at the door, then continued in a slightly calmer tone. "Isn't that what really counts, what I want to do? So what if I could be another Julius Erving, if I don't like basketball? That's what I'd tell my dad, if I could talk to him at all. But I don't think he would understand."

"But at least you *could* be what he wants, if you wanted to." Janie felt a lump growing in her throat. "I don't even have that. What my mom wants from me is just plain impossible, but she won't see it."

"Why? What does she want you to be? An astronaut?"

"A cheerleader," she said. She knew that was unfair to her mother, but she didn't care.

Henry burst out laughing. Janie stared, her face instantly bright red. Why on earth had she thought she could speak honestly to him? She turned and reached for the door.

He stopped laughing abruptly. "Wait," he said urgently, "wait. Please don't go. I wasn't laughing at you, really I wasn't."

She heard the sincerity in his voice and let go of the knob but still refused to face him.

"It's just that I've always thought cheerleaders are ridiculous," he continued. "The idea that your mother would *want* you to be one — that's what cracked me up. Does she really, though? Waving pompoms and doing cartwheels?"

"Well, no," Janie admitted, "not exactly. But she's always telling me that I have to be more social." She sighed heavily. "Do this, join that, go there. And every time I try to do what she says, I embarrass myself."

"Oh, come on," he said, "it can't be that bad."

"Want to bet?" she said with a rueful smile. "How about that art class we were both in last term? Was I popular? Come on, the truth!"

"Well . . ." Henry cleared his throat. "I don't suppose most of them even knew who you were. You always acted so shy that nobody got to know you. But if they *had*," he added, "I think they would have liked you. Why not?" He hesitated. "You seem pretty nice to me."

"Thank you," she said in a softer tone. "That

wās a nice thing to say. But you know, that almost makes it worse. It means that I created the situation myself. No, I think it must be something about me, some quality it takes to be popular that I don't have, and never will."

"Oh, come on," he repeated, "aren't you being —"

"And anyway, why should I?" she asked, interrupting him. "We're all different, aren't we? Why should I have to make myself popular if I don't want to? Isn't it just like you not wanting to play basketball?"

"I don't know if it is or not," he said slowly. "I'm happier not playing basketball. Are you happier not being popular?"

Janie was tired of having the same conversation with Henry that she had with her mother every week. But she wasn't ready to leave. Henry's portfolio caught her eye, and she changed the subject. "I looked at your drawings."

"Did you?" he said in a carefully neutral voice.

"Uh-huh. I didn't mean to be nosy, really I didn't. But once I saw the first one I couldn't stop. They're really wonderful."

His cheeks grew pink with pleasure. "Do you think so? Really? I'm glad you liked them. I've never shown them to anybody else before. I think they're pretty good, too, but I was too scared to find out what other people thought."

" 'Pretty good'? They're great! Do you want to be an artist someday?"

"Oh no." The question seemed to surprise him. "They're not meant to be artistic. They're more like notes to myself, of ideas I don't want to forget. That's why I was so upset to think that I'd lost them. It was almost like losing a diary."

"Ideas? What kind of ideas?"

"For dress designs. That's what I want to do. Here, look." He grabbed the portfolio and slid out one of the drawings. A tall, slim girl was wearing pants that billowed out, then clasped just below the knee, and what looked like a man's double-breasted jacket. The drawing was done in broad Magic Marker strokes of black, with just a touch of pale blue on the jacket and a darker blue on the trousers.

"What I wanted to remember was the line," Henry continued. With a blunt forefinger he traced the side of the jacket and the flare of the pants. "For this outfit, the color doesn't really matter much, so I just hinted at it. But in some of the others, color and texture count for a lot, so I attach a swatch of the material to the sketch."

"These are all your own designs?" Janie asked. "That's fantastic! I thought you just did the drawings. Why, these look as good as anything I've seen in fashion magazines. In fact, they're better than a lot of the things they show."

She could see her enthusiasm was starting to make him uneasy. "Thanks," he said, starting to put the page back in the folder.

"No, I mean it," Janie continued. "The way they draw clothes in magazines sometimes, they don't look like anything a real person could ever wear. I don't even look at them most of the time. I just skip over those pages and look for the photographs. At least with photos you know that somebody really put the thing on."

34

He glanced down at the drawing. "I guess it is pretty stylized," he said.

"Oh, not *yours*," Janie protested. "That's what I was saying. When I look at your drawings, they look like things that really could exist. I mean, you could almost take that sketch, sit down at the sewing machine, and make it."

He glanced across the room toward the windows. "It's funny you should say that. That's exactly what I was doing when you knocked on the door."

"Really? You were making one of your dresses? Can I see?"

"Well . . . sure, come on." He led her to an ancient Singer sewing machine, black with gold curlicues all over it, and picked up a sketch from the table. "This is what I'm working on. It's basically a chemise with a slight blouson effect at the hips and wrists. The tricky part is the side panels in a contrasting texture. I don't know how to do real tailoring yet, so I have to keep things pretty simple."

Janie studied the drawing. It showed Henry's usual tall, slim girl, this time with long, light-colored hair, in a dress that seemed to fall straight from the shoulders to the knees, but somehow suggested her figure at the same time. The color, she decided, was somewhere between oatmeal and Cream of Wheat.

"It's beautiful," she said. "But are you really going to try to make a dress like this from scratch? Without a pattern or anything?"

"I already did," he said proudly. "There it is!"

He pointed to a heap of beige cloth on the chair

next to the sewing machine. Janie went over and picked it up. Bits of thread stuck out in odd places. When she held it up by the shoulders, it looked like a cloth tube with sleeves.

Her puzzlement must have shown on her face. "It's not *finished*, finished," Henry said quickly. "I still have to clean it up and press the pleats and things like that. Do you like it?"

She hesitated.

"I know it doesn't look like much," he continued in a discouraged voice. "It's hard to get something to shape up without any way to see how it's really coming. And even when it's done, I can't always tell if it works or not. Dresses aren't made to be worn by clothes hangers, are they?"

Janie laughed at his comical way of putting it. "No, I guess not. It's not really fair to judge this way, is it? I hate to go shopping, because I can never tell by looking if it's worth trying something on. It's so embarrassing to come out of the changing room wearing something that's completely ridiculous. That's why I let my mom buy most of my clothes."

"I wondered," he said, eyeing her dark brown flannel skirt and baggy green sweater. But before she could decide if he had insulted her, he went on. "Hey, I have an idea! You don't have to, of course, but you do look like you're the right size and all. It would really help me a lot to see it the way I meant it to be seen. Would you mind?"

Janie knew what he meant, but something made her ask, "Mind what?"

"Modeling my dress for me."

"Now? Here? Me?" She searched Henry's face. He had to be joking. Why would he want to see his dress on her? Besides, what would Mrs. Monick, the home ec teacher, say if she saw them? "I couldn't!"

"Oh." His long thin face, so alive a moment before, became wooden. "Okay. I'm sorry I asked. It's just that you're a lot like the girl I imagined when I designed it. I have to do that — have somebody in mind — or I can't work. I have a whole folder of women's pictures that I cut out of magazines. When my inspiration gives out, I can look through it for more." He gave an unhappy laugh. "If my father found it, he'd probably think they were pin-ups and be proud of me!"

Janie frowned to herself. He really was serious about wanting to see the dress he designed on her. It would cost her nothing to do it. There was a screen in the corner of the room that she could change behind. It wouldn't even take her a minute to get out of her sweater and skirt and put on the dress. And it would be very helpful to Henry.

Two things persuaded her. One was Henry's comment that she looked like the girl he had designed it for. Whether he meant it as flattery or not, she was definitely flattered. The other deciding factor was her own curiosity. How could this heap of fabric look anything like that elegant, attractive dress in the drawing? She didn't think it was possible, but the only fair way to judge was to see it on someone, and she was the only candidate present.

"I'm sorry," Henry repeated. "I guess it was a

37

weird thing to ask. The dress probably isn't much anyway." He reached over to take it from her, but she moved it away.

"No, wait," she said. "I'll try it on, but only if you promise not to laugh."

"You will? Hey, that's great! But *you've* got to promise not to laugh."

He made a point of sitting down at the sewing machine with his back to her while she walked behind the screen. The dress had a fairly wide neck, so all she had to do after slipping it over her head was to button the cuffs. It felt very loose, as if she hardly had it on at all.

As she was about to go out, she hesitated, then slipped off her shoes and socks. This didn't feel like a dress that should be worn with knee socks and scuffed loafers.

Henry was waiting by a tall full-length mirror attached to the wall. Slowly, shyly, Janie walked over and stood in front of it. Side by side, she and Henry studied the reflection of her and the dress.

As if on cue, both of them broke into helpless laughter.

"You *promised*," Janie choked out.

"So did you! What's so funny anyway?"

Janie pointed at the mirror. Henry was laughing so hard that tears gathered in his eyes.

Finally both of them stopped laughing. It was a short step from laughter to a shyness that returned double-strength. "I'd better put my things back on," Janie said awkwardly. "It's getting late."

"Wait," Henry said. "It's really not as bad as it

looks. Come back to the mirror." He took her arm, led her over, and stood behind her. She felt her face grow warm under the intensity of his look.

"Got it!" In the mirror Janie watched excitement replace the unhappiness in Henry's face. "It's two things," he explained. "The neckline and the gathers at the hips. You have narrow shoulders and a wonderful long neck, but they make the dress look much too wide for you. Hold still."

He disappeared, returning a moment later with a dozen pins jutting from between his lips. "Mufnng fu ih," he said reassuringly. He picked up a pinch of material from her left shoulder, pinned it, and did the same on the right. Miraculously, the bodice, which had jutted forward like a cowl, lay flat across the top of her chest. From the waist up, the dress was beginning to resemble the drawing.

A moment later she felt his hands on her hips. Alarms began to ring in her mind. But when she looked at him in the mirror, he didn't look like someone trying to get away with something. In fact, he seemed completely absorbed in his work. He was paying no more attention to her than if she had been a dressmaker's dummy. That reassured and disturbed her at the same time.

"There!"

His exclamation drew her attention back to the mirror. She couldn't tell what he had done, but the effect was obvious. Now the dress fell almost straight to just a hint of a gather at the hips, then in soft wavy folds to the hem. The slight puffiness of the long sleeves echoed and accentuated the shape of the body of the dress. It was clearly the dress in the sketch.

"It's wonderful," she gasped. "I can't imagine how you did it."

"It's not bad," he said grudgingly, "but it's still not —" With no warning, he reached up and pulled all her hair back to the nape of her neck. Holding it bundled in one fist and lightly touching her chin with the other hand, he turned her head first to the right, then to the left. She couldn't have felt more naked and exposed than she did at that moment. His hand brushing her neck was sending showers of ice down her back.

"Don't —" she began.

He didn't seem to notice. "You've got a great face," he said. "Look at those cheekbones, and the distance between your eyes and mouth. You shouldn't hide a face like that. Just a sec. . . ." He rummaged through his gym bag and returned with a long, narrow strip of fabric. Tucking her bangs in with the rest, he pulled her hair back again, more severely, and tied it at the back. "See what I mean?" he demanded.

Janie tried to look at her reflection as if it belonged to somebody else. It was oddly easy to do. Janie Barstow never wore such interesting dresses or wore her hair back like that. Whoever the girl in the mirror was, she didn't have the kind of round, plump-cheeked, smiling face that spelled pretty and popular in Janie's mind. But she was pretty in a different way. Any less weight and she might become gaunt, but as it was, she looked,

40

well, call it interesting. Just a little bit like . . .
what?

Of course. Like the faces of the models in
Henry Braverman's drawings.

She didn't say that to him. In fact, she couldn't
say anything at all. But a hint of a smile touched
her lips, and to her amazement the girl in the
mirror changed from interesting to quite pretty!
Henry saw it, and smiled back. But Janie had already had more revelations than she could take in
one day. "I'd better change," she said and fled for
the safety of the folding screen.

"Careful of the pins," he called.

When Janie returned, her hair was down again.
Henry didn't say anything about it, but when she
handed him the dress, he looked upset. "Are you
in a big hurry?" he said. "It won't take me long to
rip out those seams and restitch them."

"What? I don't think I understand."

"The dress. You will . . . I mean, we just fitted
it to you, didn't we? And it looks dynamite,
though maybe I shouldn't say so myself. But it
looks so great on you that it wouldn't be right for
you not to have it. If you want it," he added
hastily. "I know the sewing's pretty sloppy. This
machine must be older than my grandmother."

"Want it!" Janie stopped to swallow the lump
in her throat. "I'd *love* to have it. But are you
sure?"

"It's yours," he said gravely, "but only if you
promise to wear your hair back whenever you put
it on." He picked up a seam ripper and started
working on the dress. Janie couldn't watch. Suddenly it was the most precious length of fabric in

the world, and she just knew something bad would happen to it.

To distract herself, she asked, "How did you get to use this room? Do you have special pull with Mrs. Monick?"

"Not exactly. I, ah, offered to fix this sewing machine for her last fall. She gave me a key to the room and I sort of forgot to give it back after I finished fixing the machine. That's why I was so worried when you came in yesterday. I'm not really supposed to be here at all, but it's the only place I have to work."

"Why can't you do it at home?"

"Family problems," he said, shrugging.

"I'm sorry," Janie said. "I didn't —"

"Never mind," he said, bending over the dress again. "I'd better get this done. We don't have long before the janitor gets around to this wing of the building."

Chapter
4

The wind whipping around the corner had an Arctic bite to it. Sasha tucked her chin into her collar and tugged at the door to the sub shop. A cloud of steamy air and a wave of noisy conversation rolled out at her. She paused just inside the door to pull off her mittens, rub her ears, and look around. The room was jammed. She saw people she recognized from every class and group at Kennedy, all talking and eating like crazy.

She shuddered to think of all the processed cheese, white bread, and preservative-filled meat her schoolmates were putting into their systems. If she could have her way, she would turn the place into a terrific salad bar. She'd have thirty or forty different things to heap on your green leafies, all of them equally healthful. Not that the kids would keep coming if she did; the junk food habit had too strong a hold on them.

A hand was waving from the far end of the shop. She made her way back and found Phoebe and Woody sharing a big plate of fries. It occured to her once again that the two of them would make a good couple. They had been close friends for years, they spent loads of time together, and Woody obviously adored Phoebe. But of course Phoebe was still in love with Griffin, who had dropped out of school to go to New York to be an actor. It didn't seem very likely to Sasha that Phoebe could go on loving someone she never saw, but Sasha did not consider herself an expert on the subject of love.

Woody leaned back, tucked his thumbs in his red suspenders, grinned, and said, "It's Sasha Jenkins, girl reporter! Any news?"

"Not one single new," she replied, falling in with an old joke between her and Woody. She slid onto the bench. "Hi, Phoebe. How are you?"

"Mm-wrfft," Phoebe said around a mouthful of french fries. "I was just telling Woody about our adventure during vacation," she continued after swallowing.

Sasha smiled. She had been invited to spend a weekend with Phoebe and her parents at their mountain cabin. It turned out to be a more exciting time than any of them expected.

Phoebe took a sip of her Pepsi before resuming her story. "The two of us were taking a long walk when the snow started coming down. We started back right away, but we weren't more than halfway to the cabin when it got really heavy. Sasha was right behind me, but when I looked back, practically all I could see was a sort of dark lump in all that whiteness. I was scared that I'd miss the path and get us lost, but not Sash. She just kept smiling and looking around as if I'd ordered the snow especially for her."

"I like going out in snowstorms," Sasha said. "I like the way everything gets so quiet."

"Stay out in one too long," Woody observed, "and you'll get quiet, too. Real quiet."

"It wasn't so quiet back at the cabin," said Phoebe wryly. "My dad wanted to leave right away, storm or no storm. He was in a state about some case he was working on and how he had to be back on Monday morning. Meanwhile, Mom was out in the kitchen, checking the supply of lamp oil and counting the cans of baked beans in the pantry."

"Lamp oil?" Woody said.

"Um-hum. The cabin is really primitive. It doesn't have electricity, so we use kerosene lanterns for light and a woodstove for heat. There's no phone either. And the nearest house is a mile or so away, and they're only around in summertime. The road we're on is about as wide as your driveway, so it's about the last place the snowplow gets to after a storm. That's why Dad wanted to try to leave. He knew what would happen if we didn't."

"So what happened?"

Phoebe snorted. "Just what he thought. We were stuck. First the car wouldn't start, and then when we got it started, the snow was coming down so fast that we couldn't even tell the road from the ditch. You should have heard my dad. He used a few words I'd never heard before."

45

"I don't think they were English," Sasha said.

Phoebe laughed. "They sure were Greek to me! So we gave up and went back inside, and waited for the plow to come by. We were there for *four days!*"

Woody gave a low whistle. "What did you do?"

"Oh, lots of things," Sasha said. "We sat near the fire, made cocoa and popcorn, and sang songs. And the next day, after the storm was over, Phoebe and I went out and made angels and threw snowballs at the trees. We tried to make a snowman, too, but the snow was too powdery to stick together."

"Sounds like fun," Woody observed. "I wouldn't have minded being along."

Phoebe didn't seem to notice his adoring look. "It wasn't all fun. We had to shovel the driveway and bring in wood for the fire and pump water from the well, too. And the fire always died out in the middle of the night. By morning there was ice on the water bucket. Did you ever try to wash in ice water? Brrrr!"

"But what about the way the trees looked with snow on all the branches?" Sasha said fondly. "It was like a scene from a Christmas card. And remember how much fun we had trying out those old snowshoes? I kept tripping over my own feet," she explained to Woody, "and Phoebe had to keep coming back to help me up. We must have gone about as far as from here to the street in half an hour."

"Yeah," Phoebe added. "We would have gotten a lot farther if Sash hadn't started giggling every time she fell down."

46

Sasha put her nose in the air. "That was not a giggle," she said in a haughty voice. "That was a mature, sophisticated laugh. And anyway, you were cracking up, too."

"You'd know why if you could have seen yourself flat on your back with those snowshoes waving around in the air!"

"Ladies, ladies," Woody said, grinning. "No arguing at the table, please. I'm going to get another order of fries; you want anything?"

Sasha stood up, too. A couple of months before, she had persuaded the manager to stock an assortment of herb teas. She ordered a cup every time she came in, even if she didn't want it, just to help keep him convinced. "I feel like a Red Zinger," she announced.

Woody and Phoebe exchanged a glance, then said in unison, "You don't *look* like a red zinger!"

"Phoebe does though," Woody added, glancing admiringly at her thick, red hair.

Sasha missed the glance and the point. "Really?" she said. "Super. This is my treat. I bet you like it. It perks you right up." She went over to the counter before Phoebe could reply.

"See what you've done," Phoebe said with a laugh. "I'll have to drink it, too. If it poisons me, I'll come back and haunt you."

"Promise? If I thought I had even a ghost of a chance, I'd be a happy man," Woody replied. He spoke the words lightly, as if they were a joke, but his eyes were serious.

Phoebe looked down and began to fiddle with one of the silver, cloth arrowheads sewn to the pocket of her favorite Cub Scout shirt. She loved

Woody dearly. She felt almost as close to him as to Chris or Sasha. He knew it, too. She had told him many times how much she valued their friendship. But she valued his friendship too much to even contemplate letting it become a romance. She still felt raw about the way Griffin had promised so much, then inexplicably disappeared from her life. "Pheeb?" Woody said uncertainly.

"What about those fries?" she replied. "Want to make it another jumbo order and go halvesies on it?"

"Hey, sure thing," he quickly said. He seemed happy to have a chance to do something for her, even if only to bring the plate of french fries to the table. "Do you want a soda, too?"

"No thanks. I'm supposed to be drinking Red Zinger, remember?"

By the time Sasha returned to the table with two cups of herb tea, Chris and Ted had arrived. "Well, well," Ted said, "it's Bennington's latest victim! Any further developments?"

Sasha ignored the question, but Phoebe said, "Latest victim?"

"At lunchtime," Chris explained, "we came upon Laurie being particularly nice and charming to Sasha for the second day in a row, didn't we?"

"She *was* being nice!" Sasha protested.

"Uh-oh," said Phoebe. "That's a very bad sign."

"About as bad as they come," Ted agreed gravely.

"Aw, come on, you guys, she just wanted to say

something nice about one of my articles in *The Red and the Gold*. What's wrong with that?"

"Worse and worse," Phoebe said. "Laurie Bennington doesn't give compliments, she invests them. And she expects to get a lot of interest from them, too."

Ted slapped the table. "I've got it! Now that she's been taken off WKND, she's going to try to get a gossip column in the paper. That way she'd be famous and she'd be able to get her hooks into anybody she didn't like."

Woody came back in time to overhear this. "Flash!" he said. "Sub shop torpedoes love boat. Smooth sailing over for whatsis and whosie, prominent Kennedy juniors. Read next week's paper for full details and pix."

"But we might get more readers if —" The others hooted Sasha down before she could finish her thought. Of course she wasn't going to approve of having a gossip column in the paper, whether by Laurie or anybody else. On the other hand, even if Kennedy put out the best high school newspaper in the country, it wouldn't matter if nobody read it.

While the others continued their conversation, Sasha brooded about the problem. What the paper needed was a series that everybody in school would *want* to read. Something sensational, but solid. The kind of thing everybody talked about at lunch and between classes. She had a strong hunch that she could do a story like that about the athletics department, if only she managed to worm the right sort of inside dope from John Marquette.

49

She tuned back into the conversation when she realized that was exactly who Phoebe and Ted were discussing.

"I didn't know he worked at Superjock," Phoebe was saying.

"His cousin owns the place," Ted said.

"That explains it. He came over and asked me what I needed with a slimy kind of smile. I didn't like it, but I told him anyway. Next thing, he's telling me I'll need personal fittings and he'll be happy to take care of me. Gross and a half!"

"What did you do?" asked Chris.

Phoebe laughed. "Sort of edged away and told him I had to go put a dime in the meter. I hope he didn't see me ride off on my ten-speed!"

"I hope he did," Chris said seriously. "He deserves to find out what people think of him."

"He's not —" Sasha began, then stopped in confusion. "I wish he wouldn't come on so strong all the time, but I think it's really just a big macho act."

"Come on so strong?" said Phoebe. "I'll say! He leers and makes remarks at every female above the fifth grade. He's convinced that he's what every girl wants. He's just spreading the wealth. Sasha, you're not *interested* in that big side of beef, are you?"

Sasha turned bright red. "No, of course not! But I had to promise to interview him for the paper. I mean, I want to interview him, for a story I'm working on."

"Hmmph," Phoebe grunted. "Well, do it at school, in the middle of the day in a crowded

50

place, with a few friends in calling distance, and you should be all right."

"Well, I . . ." Phoebe was exaggerating, of course, trying to alarm Sasha. She could handle someone as thick between the ears as Marquette. "I agreed to go out to dinner with him. Not a date," she added quickly, as Phoebe opened her mouth to protest. "It's purely business."

"Nothing about Marquette is pure," Phoebe said. "You're asking for big trouble."

"Come on, it can't be that bad." She turned to Chris. "Can it?"

Chris looked troubled. "I don't like spreading gossip," she said, "but I've heard some stories. Ted, didn't you tell me something about him a while ago?"

"I know Marquette pretty well," Ted said slowly. "We've played football together for a couple of years, and you know how guys talk in the locker room or on the bus after a game."

The three girls exchanged glances. They *didn't* know, but they could imagine.

"Anyway, I've heard him tell a few stories about himself that I didn't like much. It may all be a lot of hot air, but maybe not. He's proud of being the kind of guy who won't take no for an answer. The way he figures, no girl could say no to him and really mean it, so he just doesn't listen."

"But that's ridiculous!" Sasha said.

"Not if you're the girl, it isn't," Ted replied. "Which is why I think Phoebe's advice is pretty good. If you're going someplace with Marquette, stay out of dark corners. In fact, stay out of any kind of corners."

Sasha tried to tell herself that she was smart enough to handle Marquette, whatever stories Ted had heard. She could think rings around that neckless wonder. She was going to go to that dinner, do the interview, get all the information she wanted from him, and be safely home before he even knew what had hit him. Nothing could possibly go wrong.

Chapter
5

Janie dropped her books on the kitchen table and called out, "Mom, I'm home!"

From the other side of the sliding doors, her mother's voice said, "We're in here, dear."

Janie took a quick peek in the fridge, then went into the living room. Beverly and Betty, her twin sisters, were sitting on the rug near the fireplace. Bev was playing with the miniature loom she had gotten for Christmas, and Betty was reading.

Mrs. Barstow was at the far end of the sofa. The center cushion and the top of the coffee table were hidden by dozens of stacks of index cards that she was in the midst of rearranging. She pushed her reading glasses onto her forehead and looked up. "Hello, dear. Good day at school?"

"So-so." Janie plopped herself into a chair. She kept the paper bag containing Henry's dress on her lap. She was taking no chances of something happening to it.

Her mother sighed. "One of the women at the club was telling me how much easier all this would be if I used a computer. I told her that I am just technologically advanced enough to deal with the controls of the microwave, but she insisted. She very nearly had me convinced, too."

"What are you doing?" Janie asked.

"We're sending out a fund-raising letter. Everybody submitted lists of friends, relatives, and business associates, and then we put each name and address on one of these cards. Now I have to sort all of the cards by zip code."

"Can I help?"

"Why, thank you." She passed Janie a stack of cards about an inch thick. "If you'll put these in alphabetical order, any duplicates ought to turn up pretty quickly." As Janie began to shuffle through the cards, she added, "You're home late today. Were you working on the newspaper?"

Janie had not yet gotten up the courage to tell her mom she had quit the paper after that one awful afternoon. First she had decided to wait until the end of the week, then until the start of vacation, then until after New Year's. She was so reluctant because she knew what would happen. Janie had volunteered for *The Red and the Gold* in the first place to pacify her mom.

"Uh, no," she said quickly, "I stayed to help someone with a project." That was true, if misleading. She considered telling her mother about the dress, maybe even trying it on for her, but she didn't dare. First she wanted to take another look at it alone. She had to make sure that it was as

54

wonderful as she remembered. It didn't seem possible.

"That's nice," her mother replied. "I'm glad to see you're finally starting to make friends. I know it's hard to come to a new place and start over, but people are much the same anywhere. If you keep an open mind and show them that you want to be friendly, they'll respond in kind."

"Um-hum," Janie said, fingering the index card for someone named Josiah Quincy IV. Why was it so hard to remember where 'q' came in the alphabet?

"Austin," Mrs. Barstow said a few minutes later, looking at an index card. "Don't they have a daughter in your class?"

"Sure," Janie said. "Chris. There's Brenda, too — that's Chris's stepsister. She's going with Brad Davidson."

"Chris is?"

"No, Brenda." Her mother still didn't quite understand why Brad, the president of the student body, had ended up taking Janie to the home-coming dance. Janie tried to explain three or four times, but Mrs. Barstow was determined for her to take advantage of her social opportunities.

"Oh? That's something recent, isn't it? The last time I ran into Margery, she seemed worried about Brad. She said he was still depressed over his breakup with his last girl friend. What was her name?"

"Phoebe," said Janie. "Phoebe Hall. She's nice. She and Chris Austin are best friends."

"Oh?" There was a short silence while Mrs.

Barstow sorted some more cards. Then she said in a considered tone, "Why don't you ask Chris and Phoebe and that girl you work with on the newspaper to come over some night? You could have popcorn and hot cider."

Betty looked up from her book. "Can we have some, too?" she called.

"I'm sure you can if you behave yourselves while Janie's friends are here. What do you say, dear? We can even rent a VCR and a tape of some nice movie."

"Oh, I don't think so," Janie said. "They're probably busy."

"They can't be busy every night, and in any case it doesn't hurt to ask."

Janie took a deep breath. "Thanks, mom, but I guess not. I don't really know any of them very well."

"That doesn't really matter. This would be a good way to get to know them, wouldn't it? And it would be a lot of fun for you. Remember the time you had a slumber party and one of the pillows burst open? We were cleaning up feathers for weeks! It was fun, though, wasn't it?"

"Mother, I was twelve years old then!"

"Oh, I beg your pardon," her mom replied. "And now you are too mature to have fun?"

"No, it's just that —" What was the point? Once her mother got into her crusading mood, she was almost impossible to stop. "Look, those girls have been friends for years and years. Why would they want to come over here?"

"Why? To have a good time and to get to know you better, that's why." She put down the stack of cards and took off her glasses. "Look, dear, I know it's been hard for you, to come here not knowing a soul and to have to make all new friends. It hasn't been easy for me either, you know. I've felt like giving up lots of times. But what if I went up to my room and opened a book every time I faced having to do something that made me uncomfortable? That wouldn't be very smart, would it? Or very healthy, either."

Janie leaned forward, pretending to study one of the index cards. She had never really considered that the move to Rose Hill might have been hard on her mom. Her mother was strong, confident, capable, and sure of herself.

There was a pain just behind Janie's left eyebrow. She started to rub her forehead and temples.

"Do you have a headache?" her mother asked. "Why don't you give me back those cards. Reading that handwriting is too much of a strain after a full day of school. I'm almost done anyway."

"Well. . . ." Feeling like a complete fraud, Janie passed over the stack of cards. "Can I do anything in the kitchen?"

"No, no, go lie down for a few minutes. Later you can peel the carrots and potatoes."

"*I* wanted to peel the carrots," Bev said.

"You did it last time," said Betty. "It's my turn."

While her mother was arranging a coin toss to decide which twin peeled the carrots, Janie escaped up the stairs to her bedroom.

The room looked a little like a photograph of a teenage girl's room in a magazine. Janie's mother had chosen the early American pine furniture, the white curtains with a pattern of leaves and strawberries, and the matching bedspread and pillow cover. The pine bookcase held only picturebooks and old schoolbooks. The books that Janie cared about, the science fiction fantasies she read and reread until the pages started falling out, lived in her hideaway in the basement.

Henry's dress was still folded. She shook it out, held it at arm's length, and studied it doubtfully. Could this cloth really be the wonderful creation she remembered? Holding it against her body, she walked to the full-length mirror attached to the closet door. The dress still didn't look like much. Neither did she. Perhaps Henry had hypnotized her into believing that the dress was beautiful. Or she had wanted to believe it so badly that she had convinced herself.

Janie felt guilty for thinking such thoughts. She had an obligation to Henry. He had made the dress himself, with his own hands, from his own design, and had spontaneously given it to her. It deserved a fairer test from her than she had yet given it.

In the bottom drawer of her desk was a large, flat plastic tortoiseshell box. It had come free with the cologne she bought her mom for Mother's Day the year before.

She put it on the desktop and opened it. Along one side were a dozen small tablets of eye shadow in colors that ranged from dark blue to bright red. On the other side were various lip creams and lip glosses, two lip pencils, and a lip brush. The center compartment held powders, blushes, shadows, an eyebrow pencil, eyeliner, several brushes, and a tube of mascara.

Her first attempt made her look like something that had escaped from the circus. She laughed. Studying her face in the mirror, she tried to recall what Henry had said about it. She tried to recall how the girls in his drawings were made up. Putting on cosmetics *couldn't* be any harder than algebra.

On her next try, Janie limited herself to a line of eye shadow on the outer corners of her eyes, some blush along the inner part of her cheeks, and a dot of blush in the center of her chin. Once she blended them with a soft brush, she couldn't even tell that she was wearing makeup, but she knew her face looked more interesting.

Her hair was next. She brushed it back, just as Henry had done, and slipped a rubber band around it. In her dresser was a small silk square, tan with a squiggly design of red and orange, that an aunt had bought in England and given to her for her birthday. She knotted it around the ponytail and studied the effect. Henry was right: It was a mistake to wear her hair down around her face.

Now for the dress. She turned away from the mirror to put it on. She didn't want to look until she knew she was ready. It settled on her shoulders and around her hips as if it had been made for her. But then, she considered, it had been!

She swallowed a couple of times, wiggled her shoulders to loosen them, and turned around.

"It's beautiful," she whispered to herself. She stepped back, turning first one way, then the other. She looked away, then took quick glances at the mirror, as if she expected to catch the illusion before it had time to reform. But each time she saw the same thing: a tall, slim girl with striking features, modeling what had to be a designer dress. The only jarring note was the white anklets on her feet.

"Oh," Janie said. "What am I going to do for shoes?" Lifting off the dress and laying it reverently on the bed, she knelt down to rummage on the floor of the closet. She pushed aside leaky rainboots, sneakers, white sandals, bedroom slippers that looked like elephants, and three mismatched flipflops before she found what she was looking for: a pair of flats in tan leather. She had worn them once, to a cousin's wedding the previous summer. Whether they still fit or not, she was going to wear them with Henry's dress. She was going to do it the very next day, at school, before she had time to lose her nerve.

Chapter
6

Phoebe and Woody were the first to arrive at the crowd's usual lunch table. They sat down next to each other and Phoebe began to eat her salad. Woody stirred his food around on his plate and made a comic face. "You know something?" he announced. "These ravioli look like pillows for mice."

"Yuck," said Phoebe. "What an idea."

"Not only that, it wouldn't surprise me if they *have* been pillows for mice." He speared one and held it up for her to examine. "Isn't that a little bit of gray fur there?"

Phoebe refused to look. "Don't complain to me," she said. "Didn't I tell you to get the salad plate? If you keep eating pasta for lunch, you'll need those suspenders of yours, because you won't be able to find a belt that'll fit around your middle."

"Ouch!" He held up an arm as if protecting

himself from a blow. "I can't eat that rabbit food," he continued. "Gives me too much energy. Strengthens my urges. Look at how rabbits spend their time."

"Woody!" She moved sideways, avoiding the elbow aimed at her ribs. "Come on, be serious."

"Uh-uh. It's habit-forming and may be hazardous to my health."

"No, I mean it." She balanced her fork from one edge of the salad plate to the other, then tried to rest the knife across it. Both of them toppled into the greens. "Argh! Russian dressing on the handles!"

"Wait till he has his clothes on," Woody said. "Then tell him to go back to Moscow."

Phoebe paused from wiping off her knife and fork to figure out what in the world he was talking about. As Woody's pun sank in, she gave her usual appreciative groan.

"I did a lot of thinking over vacation," she went on. "You know, when we were snowed in at the cabin. There wasn't much else to do, really."

"Next time invite me. I'll keep you entertained." There was a plaintive undertone to his request.

"I'd love to if I thought you'd behave yourself."

"You mean not juggle the glassware or short-sheet your bunk?"

She gave him a straight look. "You know that isn't what I mean," she said. He lowered his eyes. "Anyhow, I did a lot of thinking. About me, and Brad, and — and Griffin."

Her voice fell almost to a whisper. It still hurt

too much even to say his name aloud. No sooner had she fallen completely in love with him than he dropped out of school and went to New York to pursue his first big break as an actor. She had understood. She had even, through the pain of parting, admired his courage and determination. But she couldn't understand what had happened next.

Griffin had asked her to come to New York for a weekend. She had agreed, even though it meant lying to her parents and convincing a friend to cover for her. He was supposed to call her Thursday night to make their final plans, but he hadn't. Nor did he call on Friday afternoon or during the evening.

That night, the night of the homecoming dance at school, she sat home by the telephone until after the Late Show ended and the TV image turned to gray fuzz. The pictures in her mind were far more vivid than anything on the screen could have been. She saw him lying in the street somewhere, beaten and robbed; or in a hospital bed with his ID and memory gone; or dancing at a trendy rock club with some beautiful, talented actress from his show.

She must have fallen asleep, because the ring of the telephone woke her up. It was Griffin, but the voice didn't sound like him. Nor did the words. All he would say was that he had to cut old ties. His new work needed all his attention. He didn't think they should see each other again, or write, or call. A clean break.

Woody's voice broke into her recollections. "Next time you talk to Griffin," he said, "be sure to tell him that he's still entitled to a Kennedy Follies jacket with his name embroidered on it. That duet you guys did was a real show-stopper."

"It seems like years ago, doesn't it?" Phoebe said with a sad, nostalgic smile.

"Not to me. I'm just starting to catch up on the sleep I missed putting that mess together. Of course, I'd do it again tomorrow if anybody asked me. And if I knew I could count on our surprise superstar, Phoebe Hall."

His praise brought a touch of color to her cheeks. She knew that his compliments were sincere. She and Griffin *had* been the surprise hit of the Kennedy Follies. Not that she deserved any of the credit. Griffin had real talent, and he had somehow drawn a performance from her that made her look talented, too.

"That was one of the things I was thinking about over vacation," she said slowly. "Looking back, I realized that being part of the show was just about the most exciting thing I've ever done. And since — well, since Griffin left town, I've been dragging around as if I'm only half alive. I don't want to go on like that. I want to get involved in something. Something that I can really contribute to. I thought you might have some ideas."

Woody leaned back and tucked his thumbs into his red suspenders. "Well-l-l, Pheeb-a-re-bop, I may have just the thing you're looking for. Maybe. The thing is, it's still up in the air. Some of us were talking the other day about how dead this part of the year is. We tried to think of ways to pep things up at dear old Kennedy High. We thought of a couple, too, but now I have to talk them over with Brad and get the point of view of student government. If any."

Phoebe heard only part of what he said. "That's another thing I thought about a lot up at the cabin," she said. "Brad. I've really got to straighten things out with him. I was the one who broke up with him, after I met Griffin, but . . . I don't know, I'd depended for so long on Brad always being there. When he suddenly started seeing someone else, it came as a big shock. Especially for it to be my best friend's stepsister!"

"Did you expect him to date a complete stranger?" Woody asked.

"I didn't expect him to date *anyone*," replied Phoebe. "I know that wasn't fair or sensible of me, but that's how it was. And something else: You remember how he kept acting, don't you? Walking past me in the hall as if I didn't exist? Getting up and leaving the room when I came in? Remember?"

"Uh-huh," Woody said reluctantly, "I remember. But you gotta remember he was really hurt."

"Oh, I do, don't worry. And I blame myself, too. Maybe I could have made it less painful for him if I'd tried harder. But that's not what I'm talking about."

Woody looked confused. "It's not?"

"No. What I'm talking about is the way suddenly, as soon as he and Brenda got together, things were supposed to be okay again. Maybe they were okay with them, but they weren't okay with me. They were pretty far from okay, as a mater of fact. And I felt completely abandoned, with no one at all to turn to."

"Phoebe!" He sounded reproachful. "You know you can always turn to me, don't you?"

Phoebe silently scolded herself for her poor choice of words. "Sure I do, Woody," she said aloud, "and it's very sweet of you to say so. But the way things were, it wouldn't have been fair of me to lean on you. Anyway," she went on quickly, before he could say any more, "it was idiotic of me to feel jealous toward Brenda. Brad was free to go out with anybody he wanted to, without asking permission from me or anybody else. Once I put it like that, I realized that I want to be friends with him again."

"I think he wants that, too," Woody said. "I'm sure he does."

"I wish I could make friends with Brenda, too. I wasn't very nice to her. I know what a rough time she's had since she came to Kennedy. She must really hate me."

"Oh, I don't know," said Woody. "I wouldn't be surprised if she really wants to like you. Have you given her a chance to? Maybe she's just waiting for some kind of sign from you."

Phoebe was about to say how much she hoped he was right when a familiar voice said, "Hey, Cardinals, let's bop till we drop!"

"Peter!" Woody exclaimed. "What are you doing here? Aren't you supposed to be doing your show? I was just telling Pheebarooni how nice and quiet it was in here today. Did you bend your needle or what?"

The school DJ put down his tray, tossed his

leather bomber jacket on a chair, and growled. "Those dorks," he said. "We've got a problem in the main control board. Nothing major; anybody with a soldering iron and half a brain could fix it, and hold his breath while he did it. But those so-called technicians from the Board of Ed. say they'll need at least a week. We'll be lucky if they take less than two, the turkeys! So I'm off the airwaves until further notice, boys and girls. Grrr!"

"Why didn't you just fix it yourself?" asked Phoebe.

"I would have, but I've got this doofus named Kevin for an assistant. He noticed the problem and reported it without telling me. That makes it official Board of Ed. business. If I touch that control board now, they can throw me off the air and hang me by my thumbs for the next fourteen years."

He looked moodily at his grilled cheese sandwich and added, "Boy, what I'd give to have Janie Barstow back! Nothing's worked right since she left the station. I can't even find one of my Bruce Springsteen albums. It's pretty rare, too: an Australian pressing with a cut on it that's never been released in the U.S."

"You should look down under," Woody said.

"Down under what?" asked Peter, puzzled.

"Just down under. An Australian record? Down under? Get it?"

Peter and Phoebe groaned, and Peter reached over to snap Woody's suspenders.

"Is this a private fight," Ted said, towering over Woody, "or can anyone buy into it?" Kennedy High's star quarterback had a tray in each hand. He set them down gently, hitched up his faded jeans, and pulled out a chair for Chris, who was right behind him.

"Hi, everybody," Chris said. "Peter! What are you doing here?"

Once again the benched DJ began to explain, and complain, about the school technicians, but this time Phoebe didn't listen. She had just noticed Brenda and Brad in the line for the cashier.

She watched them intently. Brad, as usual, looked exactly like a student body president and future Princeton student: penny loafers, neatly pressed khakis, blue-and-white striped Oxford-cloth shirt with button-down collar, and a dark crew-neck Shetland sweater. Brenda was harder to type: Her pegged black jeans said tough, but the loose white blouse with smocking and embroidery across the top said sweet and pure.

Phoebe did miss her closeness with Brad, but her romantic interest in him had evaporated long before she finally broke up with him. All she wanted was to keep him as a friend. And after reading the essay in *The Red and the Gold* Brenda had written about running away from home and discovering a halfway house that changed her life, Phoebe felt a strong sympathy for her, as well as an urge to know her better.

Brad's steadiness and commonsense gave Brenda the stability she needed. She was good for him as well, skeptical and unconventional enough to keep him from becoming too stuffy.

They had just reached the cash register. Brenda was glancing around the lunchroom as if trying to decide where they should sit. Woody had said he thought that all Brenda needed was some kind of sign from Phoebe; this was as good a time to give it as any. She waited until Brenda looked in her direction, then gave a casual wave.

Brenda glanced behind her, as if doubtful that Phoebe was waving to her. Then she leaned toward Brad and said something. Both heads turned toward Phoebe again. She waved and smiled.

The two stepped away from the register and seemed to be conferring. Or arguing. Phoebe stopped watching them. She had done what she could at this point. It was up to them now.

Woody, next to her, cleared his throat meaningfully, nudged Phoebe, and called out, "Hi, Brad, hi, Brenda. Pull up some chairs. We're plotting the overthrow of student government. You can flip coins to decide if you want to be plotters or hostages."

Phoebe looked up. Brenda was giving her a wary sideways glance. She reminded Phoebe of the small animals that browsed near the cabin, the way they looked when she leaned out her window to watch them. One wrong move, and she would break for cover. "Hi," Phoebe said, and smiled.

"Hello." Then Chris asked Brenda a question, and she turned to answer. But the tiny exchange was enough. Phoebe was satisfied. She and Brenda were not yet friends, but they were not enemies.

"I hear you were snowed in and caught a cold," Brad said casually.

Phoebe tried to be just as casual, though her heart was pounding. "Um-hum. It was fun, if you're part Eskimo. What's the latest from Princeton?"

"Well, you know that guy I met when I went up for my interview? I just got a long letter from him, full of all kinds of things he says he wishes he had known when he was a freshman."

Woody overheard. "Like where to find pizza after eleven and where the girls are," he cracked.

Ted joined in. "That's easy, the girls are off having pizza."

"That's a relief," Brenda said tentatively.

"Huh?" Woody's brow furrowed in confusion.

A sly smile spread across Brenda's face. "As long as they're not having pizza in the student government offices, I figure I'm safe," she said.

Phoebe giggled, almost choking on her soda at Brenda's unexpected humor. As the others laughed, she and Brenda shared smiles of knowledge and sympathy.

Janie clutched the towel around her and padded silently across the locker room. Her breath came quick and short, as if she had just come off the courts. She had made it safely through a morning of classes, but the real test was just about to take place. Lunch hour followed gym. If anybody was going to notice the new Janie, it would happen at lunch — but she had to make it happen.

The dress hung in her locker. The silk scarf and two or three items of makeup lay on the locker's shelf. The dress slipped on just as easily as it had that morning in her room. She collected her hairbrush, makeup, and scarf, and stepped over to a mirror. *Keep it simple*, she warned herself.

70

She brushed back her hair, fastened the scarf, and put on two small touches of blush. Blended well, they were completely unnoticeable, but they brought new definition to her face. A bit of eye-shadow and a pale lip gloss, and she was done. Once more Janie studied the girl in the mirror.

"Why, hello, Janie, how *are* you?"

Janie's heart sank. Those sugary tones could belong to only one person: Laurie Bennington, the one person she least wanted to run into at this moment.

"You look simply marvelous," Laurie gushed. "That outfit is so *hot*. Is it new?"

"Uh, no," Janie lied, "just something I had around." She didn't want to give Laurie an opening for any more questions.

"Really? I'd love to come over some day and browse through your closets. You might have some other treasures lying around." Laurie was in jeans and boots of brown leather and a shiny red blouse with a very deep V-neck. Twisted strands of seed pearls, garnets, and gold beads encircled her left wrist, and matching strands sparkled around her neck.

"Are you on your way to lunch now?" Laurie added. "We can go together."

No! Janie was horror-stricken. Today of all days, she was not going anywhere with Laurie! This was the first time Laurie had even said hello since Homecoming. Laurie had been sure she had trapped Brad into taking her to the dance, but her maneuvers had backfired. Brad had stood Laurie up, for Janie of all people. The humiliation should have made her Janie's enemy for life, but

71

here she was being friendly. *Too* friendly.

"Uh, no," Janie said faintly, "I have to do a couple of things first."

"What a shame! Tell me, are you still seeing a lot of Brad Davidson?" Laurie asked sweetly. "Someone told me that he had taken up with Chris Austin's wayward stepsister, but I don't believe in listening to gossip. I mean, how could he do that after you were his date for the most important social event of the fall?"

Janie glanced around, looking for a reason to escape. "We, ah. . . ." she began. "We weren't really, I mean —"

"It's true then!" Laurie exclaimed. "Oh, poor Janie! Men are so hateful! First Peter Lacey threw you over for that antisocial, ungrateful little skater, Lisa Chang. And now I find out that Mr. Ivy League did the same thing for the sake of a girl who brags about her sleazoid friends in the school paper. Well, never mind, you're worth a dozen of them. Come on, let's go to the cafeteria and have an old-fashioned girl-to-girl chat."

"No, really," she said, grasping the edge of her locker door, "I can't. Not today."

Laurie adjusted the collar of her blouse to deepen the vee a little more. "Oh well, another time," she said indifferently. Anyone watching would have been sure Janie had forced the conversation on her and that Laurie had put up with it solely from kindness.

As soon as she went out of sight, Janie sank to the bench and took a deep breath. That had been a narrow escape. Why on earth had Laurie sought her out like that? What had she wanted? And today, of all days!

Could that be it — Henry's dress? Did it really look stylish enough to awaken Laurie Bennington's interest? It didn't seem possible, but it was the only explanation she could think of: A simple, superficial change was all it took to receive the attention of someone who was part of the Kennedy elite.

From the cafeteria line, Janie could see that the big table in the north corner was nearly full. Maybe she should sit elsewhere today and make the experiment some other time. After all, the only thing she had *really* resolved to do was to wear the dress. And here she was, wearing it. She hadn't promised she would try to horn in on the most popular crowd in school. She may have thought of it, but she hadn't *promised*. But this adventure was like going off the high dive at the pool as a little kid: She had climbed the ladder. If she backed out, she might never try again.

Janie paid for her sandwich, picked up her tray, and walked over with her head held high. She couldn't slouch; it wouldn't have been fair to Henry's creation. As she drew closer, she saw that most of the faces around the table were familiar. Brad was there, sitting next to his new girl friend, Brenda. Janie's heart warmed as she recalled how nice he had been to her at the Homecoming dance. As if sensing her thoughts, he looked up, gave her a nod and smile of welcome, and pulled out the chair on the other side of him.

73

She put her tray on the table and was about to sit down when a voice said, "Hey, hey, it's Janie! What's happening?"

"Peter!" she exclaimed, dropping into her seat. "Peter, it's lunchtime! What are you doing here?"

Peter slapped his forehead with the heel of his hand. All the others at the table burst out laughing.

Janie looked around. What was the joke? Had she just said something dumb?

"You're number five to ask me that," Peter said with a phony pout. "What is it, nobody wants me here?"

"The show," Janie said. "What happened to the show?"

"My ratings slipped and they canned me. Just kidding," he added quickly when he saw her expression. "We're off the air for a week or so with 'technical difficulties,' that's all. See what happens when you desert the ship? I was just telling everybody how you kept the station going last fall. We're still coasting on the energy you put in."

Janie colored and looked down at her hands, but there was a smile on her lips.

Ted and Peter were soon engaged in a discussion of the differences between punk and garage rock, and the L.A. versus the Valley sound. Janie didn't bother trying to follow what they were saying. She was content to sit there, eat her chicken salad on toast, and be part of the crowd.

She was brushing the last crumbs off her fingers when Brenda leaned forward and said, "You have Mr. Sholeson for history, don't you?"

"Yes. You, too?"

"Uh-huh. Could you believe that assignment he gave us over the holidays? Some of the kids in my class wanted to write a letter of protest to the principal. We had to read almost a hundred pages," she explained to Brad, "all about the Louisiana Purchase and the Monroe Doctrine. I never did figure out what one had to do with the other."

"Not much," Janie laughed, "except that they were next to each other in the book of readings."

"Sometimes I wonder if the people who run schools ever think, or if they just keep on doing what they've always done."

"Brenda?" Janie said, feeling very daring. "You know that essay you wrote in the school paper, the one about your friend at the halfway house?"

"Yeah?" Brenda said warily. Brad, sitting between them, leaned back and became very involved with his pocket calendar.

"Well, I told you how much it moved me. You made me see him, and understand what he's doing, and why it's so important. But I wanted to say that I still find myself thinking about it. I bet I'm not the only one, either."

"I'm glad to hear that," Brenda said softly. "Thanks, Janie." In her eyes Janie could see that Brenda knew what it was like to be an outsider. They had adopted different ways to deal with it, that was all.

"What I don't understand," she continued, "was how you got up the nerve to put something so personal in print for everyone to read. I don't think I could ever do that."

"I don't think I could either," Brenda said. She

glanced down the table at her stepsister and laughed ruefully. "The first I knew about it was when I picked up *The Red and the Gold* and saw it there. By then it was already too late for cold feet."

Janie stared at her. "You didn't know? You must have been furious!"

"I was. It gave me a lot of grief." She reached over and took Brad's hand. He gave it a reassuring squeeze. "But when I found out that reading my article was helping other kids with problems, I changed my mind. Now I'm glad it got printed."

Janie excused herself to buy an ice-cream sandwich. When she returned to the table, Phoebe Hall called to her. "Janie, that's a terrific dress you're wearing."

All the others turned to look. Janie's face flushed. The girls were studying her dress, but the guys were looking at *her*.

"That's new, isn't it?" Chris asked. "It looks great on you."

"Uh, thanks," Janie said. She slipped into her chair, hoping that everybody would find something else to look at.

"Did you get it at Milovan's?" Phoebe asked. "I was there the other day, and I didn't see anything that nice."

"Don't be silly," Chris said. "She must have found it at one of the boutiques in Georgetown. Right, Janie?"

"Well. . . ." What was she going to tell them? Henry had sworn her to secrecy, but she couldn't lie about where she got the dress. It wasn't right, and she didn't know enough about fancy dress

76

shops to lie convincingly anyway. "Not really," she said. "To tell you the truth, a friend made it for me."

Phoebe said, "You're kidding! Do you know what pattern she used?"

Janie thought fast. Changing his sex seemed like a harmless way to help protect Henry's secret. "She didn't use one; she just sort of made it up. That's her hobby, designing clothes."

"That's an original design?" Chris sounded impressed. "It looks very professional. And it suits you really well."

"Your friend has a great future," Phoebe said. "Hey, do you think you could talk her into making a dress for me? How much does she charge for a dress like yours?"

Thinking fast was getting easier for Janie. "Uh, fifty dollars."

"Fifty dollars!" Phoebe exclaimed.

Janie cursed her own ignorance. She had obviously named a ridiculous figure. She had no idea what price would have been reasonable. "Well," she began, "I know that —"

"But you must have supplied your own fabric," Chris said.

Janie was growing more confused by the moment. "No, I —"

Phoebe interrupted her. "You paid fifty dollars for the whole thing? Will she make one for me at that price?"

"I don't know, I. . . ."

"And for me?" Chris said.

Brenda had been listening to all this. She caught Janie's eye and laughed. "I'll wait until another saleslady is free," she said. Janie laughed, too.

"Hey, I'm not kidding," Phoebe said. "Neither is Chris. Right?"

"Right. How about it, Janie?"

Janie was caught between excitement and dismay. Henry would flip when she told him. At least she expected that he would. But she didn't have any right to commit him to something without his knowledge.

"I'll tell you what," she said finally. "I'll write down your sizes and everything, and I'll ask hi — her if she wants to do it. I really can't make any promises. But I can tell you tomorrow what the answer is."

"Super!" said Phoebe.

"We appreciate it," Chris added.

Chapter
7

Henry's jaw dropped when he heard her news. "Fifty dollars!" he exclaimed.

"Is that all right?" Janie asked timidly. "I did tell them I couldn't promise." She had spent most of the time since lunch worrying.

"How did you decide on fifty dollars?"

She studied his expression. He looked a little stunned, but he didn't seem angry at her. "I don't know. They asked me how much I paid, and I had to say something. I don't shop for clothes much, so I didn't really know. But I figured a designer dress ought to cost more than a pair of designer jeans, right?"

"A designer dress. . . ." he said wonderingly. "I guess it really is one, isn't it? And that means that I'm a designer!"

"Then fifty is all right? It's not too little?"

"Mm, I think it's okay." He reached for a pad and pencil. "Let's see, if we figure eighteen for material and another three for zippers and thread and all, that's twenty-one. And say four more for odds and ends. Which leaves twenty-five. Oh — and commission. How does ten percent sound? I know you deserve more, but this is a tight-budget operation."

Janie backed away. "For me? Oh no, I couldn't!"

"You have to," Henry said calmly. "We've got to be businesslike about this right from the start. Sales commissions are an ordinary part of the cost of doing business."

"Really?" He nodded. She closed her eyes and tried to think of what to do. She was afraid she would offend him if she kept refusing, but she couldn't take money for doing him a favor. He had done so much more for her than she was doing for him. Then she saw a way out. "Well, if you're going to pay me commissions, I'm going to pay you for my dress."

"Oh, no," he protested, "that was a present. I can't take money for it!"

"You have to," Janie quoted. "We've got to be businesslike about this."

"Okay, okay, you win." Henry smiled. "From now on you have to pay for your dresses. At cost, of course. We can take it out of your commissions if you want." He raised a warning finger. "But the one you're wearing is still free. If you won't take it as a gift, think of it as advertising. You could even charge me model fees if you wanted!"

The way he had turned the tables on her made Janie laugh. "Okay," she said, "it's a deal."

"Now where were we?" he went on. "With your commission, each dress costs thirty dollars, which leaves me twenty. If it takes me three hours to make, that's almost seven dollars an hour, isn't it?"

"What about the time you spend designing it?" Janie asked. "Shouldn't you get paid for that, too?"

"Oh." His face fell. "I guess it's not such a great profit after all, is it? But look, I'd spend that time anyway. I *like* to do new designs. So I really shouldn't charge for it after all. Did you really get two orders, just like that?"

"Um-hum." Janie was getting over her qualms about it and beginning to feel almost smug. "And that is just the beginning. When people see Phoebe Hall and Chris Austin wearing your dresses, they'll all want one."

"Is Phoebe the girl with curly red hair?" Henry asked. "I had a class with her last year." As he talked, his right hand was sketching, almost as if it worked independent of him.

"That's her. And Chris is blond. They're both really attractive. But nice, too."

"Did you get their measurements?"

She passed over a sheet of notepaper. He glanced at it and put it in his sketchbook. "Great," he said. "Now I want you to tell me about their coloring, their personalities, what they like to do, anything you know about them. Make me *see* them."

"I'll try," Janie said haltingly, "but what for? Don't you just need to know their sizes?"

81

Henry looked at her in surprise. "I can't design dresses for them unless I know something about them."

"Design dresses?" It was her turn to be surprised. "They said they wanted one just like mine."

He dropped his pencil and put his hands on her shoulders. Once again she felt that unfamiliar thrill down her spine. "Janie," he said, "your dress was meant to be worn by someone tall and slim. Someone like you. It would look all wrong on somebody like Chris or Phoebe who doesn't have a model's figure. They need a completely different look."

"But *this* is what they ordered."

A stubborn expression settled on his face. "I don't care. I won't make that dress for anyone with measurements like theirs. In fact, now that I've seen it on you, I won't make that dress for anyone else at all. That design is yours and yours alone!"

A part of Janie's mind was memorizing all the nice things Henry was saying about her, to replay as she was going to sleep that night. The other part was beginning to wonder what Phoebe and Chris would say.

Henry seemed to read her thoughts. "Look," he said, "I don't know if my designs are any good. *I* think they are, but I don't *know*."

"Of course they are!" Janie said fiercely.

"Well then, if your friends like this dress, they'll like theirs even better, right? Because they'll be designed to suit *them*."

"Um, I guess so," Janie said. But she foresaw some explanations on her part.

"And if they don't like what I make for them," he said with a flourish, "they don't have to take them."

Janie was amazed to see what a difference the two dress orders had made in him. He seemed much more confident and self-assured. Even his posture had changed. He was standing straight, all six-foot-two of him, and holding his head high. He no longer looked furtive, like someone who was hiding a shameful secret.

But even as she was admiring the change, she saw the confidence drain from him. "What is it?" she said in alarm. "What's wrong?"

"I don't know what I was thinking about. I can't do the dresses for your friends. I'm sorry."

"What do you mean, you can't? Don't be silly! Why not?"

"I just can't, that's all!" He took a deep breath and said in a quieter tone, "Look, just before you came by this afternoon, the janitor unlocked the door and looked in. He didn't say anything to me, but I know he was suspicious. If I get in trouble with the school officials, it'll all come out, what I've been doing. I can't risk it. I'm going to have to stop using this room."

"Gee, that's too bad. I guess it's been really handy to be able to come here like this. But what does that have to do with Phoebe's and Chris's dresses?"

"Don't you understand?" he asked. "Where can I work? At home? I can't even leave my sketchbooks at home! I'm afraid my dad might go into my room looking for something and find them. You'll have to tell your friends no. I would love to do it, and it would have been a break for me, too. But there's no way. I can't afford the risk."

Janie couldn't stand to see the disappointment on his face. There had to be some way she could help. Then she saw it. "Henry?" she said timidly. "We have a sewing machine at home. I think it's a good one; it's pretty new, anyway. We even have one of those dummies that people pin dresses to. You could work there if you wanted to."

Henry's face lit up, then darkened again. "Thanks, Janie, that's really sweet of you, but I couldn't. I'd just be in the way. Your parents wouldn't agree to it."

"Sure they would," Janie insisted. "All the sewing stuff is down in the basement, in the rec room. I'm the only one who ever goes down there anyway, and *I* won't mind having you."

He looked at her doubtfully, not quite daring to believe her.

"Look," she added forcefully, "why don't you come home with me right now? We'll ask my mom and see what she says. But I know what she'll say. After she sees me in my new Henry Braverman original, she'll probably ask you to make a dress for her, too!"

"Well, if you really think. . . ." His excitement showed in his face. "It would be so great if I could. Just think, I wouldn't have to carry everything back and forth with me every day. And I wouldn't have to stop just when I was getting started. Maybe I could even come over and work on week-ends sometimes. I wouldn't make any noise," he added hastily.

"It wouldn't matter if you did," Janie said with a laugh. "You could practice drums in our basement without bothering anybody. Come on, let's go."

"Wait, I have another idea. Before we go to your house, why don't you come with me to the mall? You can help me pick out material for your friends' dresses."

"Me? I don't know anything about material. Besides, I don't know what the dresses are going to look like."

"Never mind that," he said. "I'll sketch them for you on the bus!"

Janie stopped just inside the door of Fabric Mart and looked around in a daze. Along the walls, shelves stretched to the ceiling holding bolt after bolt of material. There was every color and pattern she could imagine, in fabrics meant for curtains and upholstery, as well as clothing. Folded lengths of material were heaped high on tables down the center of the shop, under big signs announcing special sale prices on remnants. Janie brushed her fingertips across a piece of plum-colored velveteen and sighed.

"Why, Henry!" A middle-aged woman came toward them with a smile. "I was just thinking about you the other day. I've put two or three books of samples aside for you. They're last fall's colors, I'm afraid, but you may find a few nice things in them."

"Thanks a lot, Mrs. Boyne. This is Janie

Barstow, a friend of mine from school."

"Hello, Janie. That's a very attractive dress you're wearing. I don't have to ask where you got it, because I recognize the material. Our young friend here is very talented, isn't he?"

"I think so," Janie said with a shy glance at Henry.

He was blushing furiously. "Well, I. . . ." he said, almost tongue-tied, "I couldn't have gotten anywhere without your help, Mrs. Boyne. She not only taught me about fabrics," he explained to Janie, "she showed me patterns and explained the reasons for all the different technical tricks. And then after I made my first dress, we went over it and she helped me see where I'd gone wrong and how I could have done it better. Drawing clothes is easy, but making them is something else."

"Oh, no," Mrs. Boyne said. "You had the feel for it long before you met me. I just helped it along a bit. What can I do for you today?"

Henry explained that two classmates had liked Janie's dress so much that they ordered dresses for themselves. He waited pink-faced through Mrs. Boyne's congratulations, then said, "I'd like to use that medium-weight cotton blend we were looking at the last time I was here. It looked like it would drape well."

She gave a worried glance in Janie's direction. "I don't think we have any left in sand," she said. "Would you like me to look in the back?"

"Oh, no, thanks." Henry grinned. "We don't want all the girls in Kennedy High School wearing the same color dress, do we? Let's go see what there is."

Janie followed him and Mrs. Boyne to the back of the store. They had talked about colors on the bus. He had even asked her advice, but talking about colors and seeing them were not the same. Henry stopped in front of a case that contained at least three dozen bolts of the fabric, each in a different shade.

"One of the girls is blond, blue-eyed, all-American," Henry said. "For her, I'll want a blue a little more saturated than cornflower, but not quite royal." He ran his hand up the stack of fabrics and stopped at one. "Here." He slid the bolt out six inches. "Janie? Is this it?"

"Golly." She looked carefully at the material. She could see that the color was different from the pieces above and below it, but she wasn't sure which of them was closest to the color of Chris's eyes. She wasn't sure that she could have said even if she had had Chris standing right there. "I think so," she said cautiously.

"Good enough. Her eyes will pick up enough of the color when she wears it to make a perfect match." He took down the bolt of cloth and handed it to Mrs. Boyne. "I'll need two and a half yards of that one, please. And I see our redhead in a hunter green, sort of subdued, without any olive in it. Something like this, right, Janie?"

This time she had no difficulty. Phoebe would look gorgeous in that shade. Janie felt a twinge of envy. "Uh, sure," she said hastily. "That looks just right."

"Then all we need is matching thread and a few odds and ends, and we're set!"

As they walked through the mall toward the

exit by the bus stop, Henry put his free arm loosely around Janie's shoulders. She fought to keep her neck relaxed and looked sideways at him. When she was working at the radio station, Peter used to reach up and put his arm around her sometimes. When she finally realized that he didn't mean anything by it, she felt like a total fool.

Henry was looking straight ahead. He didn't even seem aware that they were touching. It *was* purely casual, then. A few moments later he took his arm away.

Chapter
8

The January White Sale at *Milovan's*, in the
Rose Hill Mall, includes dramatic markdowns on a
fabulous selection of jeans, tops, and mega-now
jackets. And if you're Georgetown-bound, drop by
Rezato to see the very latest and greatest by the most
exclusive designers, all at post-holiday prices. And
when you go, be sure to say that you saw it here in
The Red and the Gold. Support the merchants who
support your school — you'll be glad you did!

S asha Jankins cranked the sheet of paper out
of the battered Underwood typewriter and read it
over. Her nose wrinkled in disgust. She hated writing these articles. They were nothing but thinly
disguised advertisements. But the newspaper had
to sell ads to survive, and the people who bought
the ads expected a little something extra for their
money. So once a month she made a few phone
calls, gritted her teeth, and wrote her "Boutique
Scenes for Teens" column.

It could have been worse. When she first joined the paper, the editor assigned her to write a review of a new fast-food restaurant that had opened up near school. He made it clear that this was a test of her journalistic potential.

She had taken the assignment very seriously and done a thorough job. She found out the levels of carbohydrates, saturated fats, sugar, and salt in the most popular dishes and explained why each of these was bad for you. She analyzed the cost per gram of protein and showed it was a lot higher than in some other easily available foods. Finally, she awarded the place four Empty Calories for the food and three Plastic Forks for atmosphere.

It took her more than an hour to peck out a perfect copy of the article. She counted twice to be sure that it was just the length the editor had asked for. Then she tiptoed up to his desk, put it in the In basket, and fled. She couldn't bear to wait for his reaction.

The Red and the Gold came out on Friday. All morning she kept glancing out the window to see if the van had brought the papers from the printer. Finally it was there. The minutes until the next class break seemed to last forever. When the buzzer sounded, she beat the others to the door, grabbed a paper from the bundle in the hall, and found a deserted nook in the quad.

The restaurant review took up most of page five. She admired the layout and the space given to it. Then she saw the headline: BURGERS, PIZZA, AND ALL THE REST . . . AND IT'S ALL THE BEST! In disbelief she read and reread the article. It praised the food, the service, the "friendly and informal setting," and the attitude of the management "who are determined to become a solid and important part of the Rose Hill community." As far as Sasha could see, not a single word of her review had been printed. All her research, all her work had been thrown away.

It was the following Wednesday before she dared show her face in the journalism room. The moment she walked in, the editor shouted, "Jenkins! Come here, I want to talk to you!" She fought down an urge to turn and run away. "Listen," he said when she reached his desk, "what was that garbage you handed me last week? I had to stay late reworking it."

"It was a restaurant review," she said faintly. "The place is awful. I wanted to explain why."

"The place is an *advertiser*, Jenkins. Haven't you ever heard the saying, 'If you can't say anything nice, don't say anything at all?' We don't go around blasting our advertisers."

He was a senior, and the editor, and she was a lowly frosh, but her parents had raised her to think for herself and speak her mind. "But you didn't say nothing," she protested. "You said the place is good, and it isn't. It's junk."

"Well, it. . . ." He looked a little uncomfortable. "That's just your opinion, isn't it? It sounds okay to me. Besides, it's the policy of the paper to encourage new business in our area. This is a new business, and my review is my way of encouraging it. Right, Jenkins?"

"Right." Her choice was clear: Get along with him or quit the paper. After that she turned down controversial assignments unless she got a pledge from whoever was in charge that her viewpoint would be respected.

Now she was managing editor and editor-elect, and was beginning to see that the key to running a newspaper was the ability to know which compromises you could live with, and which you couldn't.

For instance, as soon as she was in charge, she meant to introduce a column called Natural Living. It would feature straight talk and information about foods, vitamins, and other issues related to health. If some readers didn't like it, they could skip over it. And if some advertisers didn't like it, they could go soak their heads in Dr. Bronner's Peppermint Soap.

On the other hand, she was still planning to sell as much advertising as she could to Roy Rogers, O'Malley's Pizzeria, and the sub shop, whatever she personally thought of the food. If she could manage to land an ad for one of the national brands of soft drinks, it would cheer her up for a week. And she was definitely going to continue writing her "Boutique Scenes for Teens" — unless she could unload it onto some unwary freshman or sophomore!

"Sasha, you're so wonderfully industrious! I've been standing here watching you work. I really admire concentration like that."

"Oh, hi, Laurie, how's it going?"

Laurie twisted the garnet-and-pearl bracelet on her wrist and sighed dramatically. "Not very well, I'm afraid. Sometimes I think I should simply stop trying and let the unimaginative little minds have their way. But that wouldn't be right, would it?"

"No, I guess not," Sasha replied, though she wasn't sure who the little minds were or why they shouldn't have their way.

"I knew you'd understand! Anyone capable of writing a beautiful article like yours was bound to understand. When I opened the door and saw you at the typewriter, looking so intent, I just knew that you were writing another article full of insight and understanding. I'm right, aren't I?"

Sasha glanced down at "Boutique Scenes for Teens." "Not really," she said. "I was doing something pretty ordinary. Most newspaper work is."

"But then a big story comes along, and that makes it all worthwhile. I know." She pulled a chair over next to Sasha's desk and sat down. "Tell me, do you ever come across a really big, important story that you know you'll never be able to print?"

Sasha's journalistic nose twitched. Laurie was not making casual conversation; she was leading up to something. "I guess that happens now and then," she replied carefully. "But if a story is important, there would have to be an awfully good reason to make us decide not to print it."

"Even if it offended powerful people or showed them in a bad light?"

Sasha quoted a sentence she had memorized from an article about the first amendment. " 'Public figures choose to step into the spotlight; they have no right to complain if its glare reveals their warts.' What powerful people are you worried about offending, Laurie?"

"Me?" She placed her hand on her chest. "I'm

not the one who ought to be worried." She leaned forward. "I have this strong feeling I can trust you. Let me tell you what happened."

"This is on the record, you know," Sasha warned. "That means I can use the information you give me and attribute it to you."

"That's all right." A vindictive expression flashed across Laurie's features, disappearing so quickly that Sasha wasn't sure she had seen it. "All I want is fair play and credit where credit is due. You know that I am the student activities officer of student council?"

Sasha nodded. Laurie had mentioned the fact the last time they met.

"Well, I've been racking my brain for weeks, trying to come up with some activity to get students more involved. January is such a low point for most people, isn't it? And then I had a really *hot* idea: a student-run fashion show. Not just boring dresses, but clothes for guys, too. The cousin of a friend of mine owns the finest sporting goods store in the Washington area, and I got him to agree to cooperate." She paused. "What is it, Sasha?"

Sasha realized her surprise must have registered on her face. "Nothing," she said hastily. "Go on." So Laurie was a friend of John Marquette.

"I was planning to come to you, to ask for help in approaching your other advertisers. Then it happened. I still don't quite know how."

"What happened, Laurie?"

"My idea was *stolen!* I suddenly learned that *my* fashion show is going to take place this month, run by Woody Webster, of all people! What in the world does he know about fashion?"

"He's had a lot of experience running shows," Sasha pointed out. "The Kennedy Follies last fall was a real success."

Laurie ignored this. "I even went up to him today and offered to help," she went on, in a voice that would have etched stainless steel. "He told me everything was under control. Under control! Under *his* control, was what he meant!"

"I don't understand. Who is sponsoring the show?"

"Student government, supposedly, but we both know what *that* means. It means darling Brad, his trashy girl friend, her pure-as-snow stepsister, and the whole bunch of them."

Sasha examined Laurie curiously. Laurie must have known that Chris was a good friend of hers. For that matter, most people would say that Sasha was part of what Laurie was calling "the whole bunch."

"But you were planning to have student government sponsor the show, weren't you?" Sasha asked.

"Sure, but *I* was going to organize it. I had some great ideas for publicity, too. That was another thing I wanted to get your expert advice on. But now it looks as if my only connection with the show will be sitting in the audience. If I bother to come."

Sasha tapped her pencil rhythmically on the desktop. "Gee, Laurie," she said after some thought, "I don't quite see what you expect me to do. The paper always does its best to publicize school events, of course, but that's not what you're after, is it?"

Laurie leaned closer again. "What I want you to do is let Brad Davidson know that *you* know the show was my idea. That *The Red and the Gold* won't just stand by while a student's rights are trampled on. That unless I am made director of the show, the newspaper will expose these abuses for what they are!"

"Um," Sasha said. "Right. Well, Laurie, I appreciate your coming by this afternoon. I'll look into all this and see what I can dig up. If something's been going on that the student body ought to know about, we'll do our best to tell them."

Laurie grabbed her forearm and squeezed. "I *knew* I could depend on you," she said. "Oh, by the way," she added as she stood up, "are you any relation to the Jenkins who run that charming bookshop?"

"Sure, that's my mom and dad. Why?"

"I never made the connection before, that's all. It's a wonderful place, so warm and inviting."

Sasha wondered uncharitably when Laurie ever had been in the bookshop to find out how warm and inviting it was. She didn't seem like a serious reader.

"I just had a *wonderful* idea," Laurie said. "A few weeks ago my father mentioned at dinner that he is planning a new program about books. He owns a cable station in Washington, you know. We ought to get him and your father together. You can never tell with that kind of thing, can you? Your father might be the perfect person to do a weekly TV show on books, don't you think?"

Sasha was privately convinced that her father was the perfect person to do just about anything; certainly anything that had to do with books. "That's possible, I guess," she replied. "I don't know if he'd like the idea, though."

"Of course he would," Laurie gushed. "*Everybody* wants to be on television. And it would be terribly good for his business, wouldn't it?" She looked up at the wall clock. "Is it really that late? It's been just great talking to you, Sasha, but I have to run. My little Mustang gets lonely sitting out there in the parking lot. Can I drop you anyplace?"

Sasha shook her head. "Thanks, but I've got more to do here." One thing she meant to do was start checking out Laurie's peculiar story about her role in the upcoming fashion show.

"Sure. I really admire your dedication. It's too bad more students don't realize how much work goes into putting out a top-notch school newspaper like ours. Well, *ciao*. Don't forget to talk to your father about the new TV show."

After the door hissed closed behind Laurie, Sasha sat back, stared at the ceiling, and chewed on her pencil eraser for several minutes. Then with a sigh she straightened up and began marking her boutique piece for the printer.

Chapter
9

As she and Henry turned onto her block, Janie began to feel uneasy. She had been so involved in their conversation on the bus trip back, she hadn't had time to worry about what lay just ahead.

"I'd better warn you about my mom," she said abruptly. "This time of day, she's bound to be home."

Henry stopped in the middle of the sidewalk and turned to face her. "I thought you said she would like the idea."

"Hm? Oh, sure. She won't mind at all. I meant warn you about what she's like."

"I give up," he said. "What's she like?"

"She'll be very glad to see you. She's always encouraging me to invite people over. She thinks I don't make a big enough effort to meet people." Janie frowned in concentration. "Her big thing right now is student activities. Why don't I try out for this? Why don't I get involved in that? Why don't I go on the school ski trip? Why don't I do more things with the other students?"

"I give up," Henry repeated, laughing. "Why don't you?"

"I've tried. But every time I do what she tells me to do, it's pure disaster. She has all these ideas about what you're supposed to do in high school. I think she gets them from magazine articles.

"Oh well," Janie said, "we can't stand around in the cold all afternoon. Come on, the sooner we get there, the sooner you'll see what I mean."

Mrs. Barstow was in the kitchen looking overwhelmed by the results of the day's shopping trip. The boxes, jars, and cans covered the table and overflowed onto the counter. "Hello, dear," she said as Janie came in. "The supermarket was out of chocolate chip ice cream, I'm afraid. I got plain chocolate instead. I hope that's all right."

"Oh, sure," Janie said in a flat tone, "that's fine." Her mom had a fixed idea Janie couldn't get along without Breyer's chocolate chip ice cream. Like a lot of her mom's ideas about her, it had been more or less true once upon a time. "Mom, I'd like you to meet a friend of mine from school. This is Henry Braverman."

"Hi, Mrs. Barstow," Henry said with a wave.

"Hello, Henry. Welcome."

Janie hung her brown jacket on a peg by the door and was about to ask about using the sewing machine when her mother said, "Is that a new dress, Janie? I don't recall seeing it on you before."

"Do you like it?"

"Why, yes, it's very attractive. But when did you ever get it?"

Janie decided on the direct approach. "Henry made it."

"Really?" Her mom clearly was confused. "How interesting. Where did you find the pattern, Henry?"

"He didn't use one," Janie replied. "He's a designer. You know, like Halston or Calvin Klein. This is a Henry Braverman original."

"Is it really? Why, Henry, you have quite a talent. Have you been interested in fashion design for long?"

Henry looked tongue-tied. Janie was about to break in and rescue him when he managed to say, "Yes, ma'am, for a long time. But I just started trying to make my designs into dresses last fall. This is the first one I feel really good about."

"Well, you certainly should feel good about it," Mrs. Barstow said. She had apparently decided to give full approval to Henry's activities. "If you ask me, that's a dress that any experienced professional could be proud of. And it certainly suits Janie. Once the word about you gets around, you're not going to have very much free time."

Janie saw a perfect opening. "That's what I wanted to ask you about, Mom," she said in a rush. "You see, I wore Henry's dress at school today, and two girls who liked it ordered dresses for themselves, and I told Henry he could use our sewing machine. That's all right, isn't it?"

"Our sewing machine? Why, I suppose so. But why not use the one he made your dress on?"

"I would, ma'am," Henry replied, "but the machine I've been using belongs to the home ec department. The only time I can work is when no one else needs it. And I don't think they'd like me to start any big projects on it."

"I see." She looked from Janie to Henry and back to Janie again. "Well, of course, in that case you're welcome to use it. Now let me see: I'm sure the manual is in the drawer. I don't know if you'll need any of the fancy attachments like the button-holer. I've never found any use for them myself, but they should be in a box on the shelf next to the sewing table. Will you need shears?"

"No, ma'am, I brought my own."

"Good. Ours aren't as sharp as they might be. I can't think what else, but if you run into any problem with the machine, just ask and I'll try to help if I can."

Janie impulsively gave her mother a hug.

"Thanks, Mrs. Barstow," Henry said. "I really appreciate it."

Janie flicked on the lights and saw the basement rec room as it must appear to a stranger. The carpet was dusty. The science fiction book she had been reading lay face down on the floor next to the overstuffed floral print couch. An uneven pile of similar books teetered on the edge of the lamp table, which also held a glass and an empty corn chips bag. Her old green sleeping bag, which served as a blanket, footwarmer, and all around security object, waited at the end of the couch.

Henry didn't appear to notice the general furnishings. He brushed past the huge couch, skirted the gray file cabinets overflowing with her dad's old business records, and stood looking at the sewing corner. This consisted of the sewing machine, built into a standing cabinet; an old metal-topped dinette table used for laying out and cutting material; the dressmaker's dummy Janie had mentioned to him; and a low bookcase full of old dress patterns, worn-out and torn garments, and miscellaneous junk. To Janie, it all looked pretty dismal.

"Do you think it's okay?" she asked timidly. "We can shift things around if you like."

"Okay? It's fantastic! It's just what I've been longing for!" He dropped the packages on the table and took the cover off the sewing machine. "Look, it's even a free arm machine! That'll make setting in sleeves about twenty times easier!"

He turned around, picked Janie up by the waist, and whirled her through the air.

"Stop it," she called through the laughter that bubbled from her. "You'll make me dizzy!"

"Oh. Sorry," he stammered. He carefully set her down and took a step backward. "I guess I got carried away."

A wave of shyness flooded through Janie and made her face grow hot. She dropped her eyes and turned away.

"Wow, it's getting late," Henry said. "I'd better get to work. Would you like to help?"

"Oh, I couldn't! I wouldn't know what to do!"

"That's all right, I'll tell you as we go along." He found the tissue paper he had bought at the mall and cut off a piece about eight feet long.

"What's that for?" Janie asked.

"We have to plan the dress before we start cutting," he explained. "When we're done, we'll have something just like a pattern, but instead of buying it, we're making it ourselves." He taped the sketch of his dress for Chris to the paneling over the sewing machine and picked up a soft pencil.

"I thought you wanted the tissue for wrapping the dresses when they're done," Janie confessed.

"No," he said seriously, "we'll use softer tissue for that." He began to draw on the tissue, outlining the different pieces of cloth that would be assembled into the dress. As he worked, he explained what each piece was for and where it would go, but somewhere in the middle Janie stopped understanding his explanations. It didn't matter. She was content to stand there, holding down the end of the tissue paper. She felt wanted and needed and useful.

"Is that all there is to it?" she asked, when Henry put down the pencil and picked up his scissors.

"Don't I wish!" he replied with an amused grimace. "No, after I cut out all the pieces, I pin them together on the dummy and find out how many dopey mistakes I've made so far. Eight is about normal. Then after I try to fix the mistakes, I pin the pieces together again and find a few more. With any luck, I'll catch almost all of them before I start cutting the material. That's why I do it this way: Tissue paper is a lot cheaper than fabric."

"Janie?" her mother called from the head of the stairs. "Can I see you up here for a minute?"

Janie and Henry exchanged concerned glances.

Had Mrs. Barstow decided not to let Henry use the basement after all? "Coming," Janie shouted.

But Mrs. Barstow was waiting with a plate of oatmeal raisin cookies and two glasses of milk on a tray. "Do you think Henry would like to stay for dinner?" she asked in an undertone. "Your father had to stay in town for a meeting, so there's plenty of food."

"I don't know," Janie said doubtfully. "I'll ask him."

Henry looked up from his pattern-cutting as she was putting the tray down. "Hey, great!" he said. "I kind of skipped lunch today. Careful," he warned, as her milk threatened to spill onto the tissue pattern. She put the glass down and sat on the sofa. He followed her over and sat down on the arm, munching a cookie. "I think your mom is nice," he continued. Janie frowned but didn't say anything. "At least she wants you to be happy. I wish my father was like that. He doesn't care if I'm happy or not, as long as I keep up the family tradition."

Janie sat up. "Family tradition?" she said.

"Do you know who my father is?" he demanded.

"Sure. He's Henry Braverman, Senior. He told me so himself."

"He's head football coach at Rose Hill State. Not only that, when he was in college, he nearly made All-American. He manages to mention that to anybody who talks to him for more than ten minutes. Get the picture?"

"You mean he wants you to play football?"

Henry scowled. "He's not that crazy. He can see I don't have the build for it. But he expects me to be a gung-ho jock of some kind. In fact, he insists on it."

"Oh!" She recalled her odd conversation with Henry's father, the day she had tried to return his portfolio. "Basketball practice!"

Henry blushed. "Uh-huh. Last year I told him I was doing cross-country. That worked great. I was never anywhere he could check on for practice, and the last thing he wanted to do on a weekend was go somewhere and watch a bunch of skinny guys running up and down hills. But this fall he told me I had to go out for a team sport. I needed to learn the importance of team spirit, according to him. So I told him I was going out for the basketball team."

"You didn't! Did he believe you?"

"Sure. Why not? I probably could make the team if I wanted to. I just don't want to. But there was no way to tell him that."

"But he'll find out! What if he comes to a game? Or talks to some guy who really is on the team?"

He shrugged. "I've been lucky so far. When it finally happens, I don't know what I'll do."

Chapter
10

When Phoebe arrived at the school lunch-room on Monday, the only one at the crowd's table was Peter. He had his headphones on and was sitting back, eyes closed, snapping his fingers in time to a tune only he could hear. She took the seat across from him and tried to guess the song from watching his fingers. She gave up after half a dozen bars.

After stirring the fruit up from the bottom of her yogurt, Phoebe opened the spiral notebook she was using to keep track of details. She had been interested when Woody told her the plans for a Kennedy fashion show, and flattered when he asked her to be a co-organizer. Then she began to realize how much work it involved.

She had spent all of her morning study hall calling department stores and boutiques, asking them to lend clothes for the show. Of the fourteen possibilities on her list, she had managed to get through to the right person in nine cases. Two had said that her request was against store policy and four had advised her to get in touch with the manufacturers instead. That left three places that were ready to cooperate — one department store and two boutiques. There wasn't much time to find others; the show was scheduled for the following Tuesday, only eight days away.

She put stars next to the stores that had agreed and arrows pointing to the ones she still had to call back, then turned to the next page. Mrs. Monick, the home ec teacher, had named half a dozen students whose designs she thought should be in the show. So far Phoebe had tracked down three, all of whom instantly said yes. One of them, a senior named Kathy, had even been wearing one of her creations, a crocheted vest, when Phoebe spoke to her. Of the other three, two were in Mrs. Monick's 2:05 class. Phoebe made a note to drop by at the end of the period and speak to them.

"Dear Diary," a familiar voice said, "had lunch with a glamorous, out-of-work DJ today and didn't say a word or look at his handsome face the whole time."

"Hi, Peter," she replied without looking up.

"You working on the fashion show bit?"

"Yup. Every time I get one problem taken care of, three more show up in its place. I hope Woody's having better luck with his assignments."

"Assignments?" Woody said from behind her. "Gee, I'm sorry, Miss Hall. I had it all done and ready to turn in, but my dog chewed it up." He took the seat next to her. "Whew!" he added.

"You wouldn't believe the trouble I'm having getting guys to model in the show. You'd think I was asking them to volunteer as practice cases at a dental school!"

Phoebe smiled. She was having just the opposite problem: trying to keep every girl at Kennedy High from appearing in the show. "Here's Ted and Chris," she said. "How about asking him?"

"Oh, I did. He tried to refuse, but Chris wouldn't let him. She appealed to his school spirit. I think that's what it's called, anyway."

"I bet I know what you're talking about," Ted growled as he pulled out chairs for Chris and himself. "I warn you, Woody, if you make me wear a necktie, I'll *wrap* it around your neck afterwards."

Woody hid his head behind Phoebe. "Oh, save me," he said in a quavering falsetto.

Phoebe pushed him away. "Come on," she demanded, "are you a man or a mouse?"

For an answer, he twitched his nose and upper lip and made a grab for her Swiss cheese sandwich. As the laughter died down, he said, "Did you ask Peter about music yet?"

"That's two pages later on my list," Phoebe replied. "Ask him yourself. He's right there."

"Peter?" Woody said.

"Yeah, man," said Peter.

"Music for the fashion show?"

"Yeah, man, I can lay it on ya," Peter said in his best exaggeration of his celebrity DJ voice.

"See?" Woody said, turning to Phoebe. "That wasn't hard, was it?"

Janie gave herself a last check in the locker

room mirror. On Friday she had run into Chris and told her that she would have the dresses for her and Phoebe on Monday. She did, too; the two boxes were in a shopping bag by her feet. She probably could have delivered them between classes, but somehow that seemed too casual. Phoebe and Chris were Henry's first real clients, and Janie had a strong desire to make the delivery an *occasion*. As part of that, she wanted to be sure to look good herself.

She had trouble recognizing the girl in the mirror. First of all, there was the hair. Henry had practically ordered her to wear it back, off her face, and suggested that she practice putting it in a French braid. It had taken a dozen tries before she began to get the knack of bringing the new strands into the braid evenly, and keeping it straight.

Not that she was going to be keeping it that way for long. Henry also had definite ideas about how her hair should be cut. When he offered to come along and instruct the stylist, Janie had immediately telephoned for an appointment. She was disappointed to learn she would have to wait until Wednesday afternoon.

Henry also had taken a break from working on the two dresses to go through her closet with her. After all, she had to have something to wear besides her new tan dress. It mortified her to look at her wardrobe through his eyes. She suddenly realized something she should have seen long before. Most of the clothes she habitually wore were drab. And she had *chosen* to dress that way.

There hadn't been very much for him to work

with, but he did manage to suggest four or five combinations that had some flair. She was wearing one of them today: a white Oxford-cloth shirt beneath an argyle sweater she had stolen from her father's closet, over a pair of blue jeans. Henry had shown her how to wear a belt over the sweater to give it some shape. And a new coat of polish had done wonders for her old loafers.

She nodded in approval. The girl in the mirror had obviously given some thought and care to her appearance. She looked interesting and attractive.

After a final glance and a tug to straighten the collar of the shirt, she picked up the shopping bag and headed toward the cafeteria.

Instead of going through the line, she went straight to the table where the crowd was assembled. Lunch could wait until she had taken care of business. This time Peter was the first to see her. He waved and gave her a smile that put a twinkle in his green eyes. She smiled and waved back.

Some of the others looked around and nodded to her. Then they went back to what they had been doing, as if her presence was such a usual thing that it was hardly worth notice. Once she would have felt ignored and hurt. She would have hovered nearby, afraid to intrude, waiting for an invitation. Now Janie understood that the others were not rejecting but accepting her. They were telling her that she was simply one of the crowd.

At least one person, however, was giving Janie special notice. Peter hooked his foot under the chair next to him and slid it out for her. As she sat down, he said, "Hey, Janie, how's the girl?"

"Okay," she said. "How about you?"

He scowled. "I feel like my brains are going to bubble out through my ears, I've got so much steam up. If they don't get me back on the air pretty soon, I'll probably take the whole darn school with me when I blow!"

Janie remembered helping Peter do his lunchtime show. He was always in motion, talking a blue streak, bouncing in his seat, boogying back and forth between the record library and the turntables. By the end of the show, she was wiped out just from watching him, but he seemed recharged by it. Doing without it had to be really rough on him.

"It won't be long, will it?" she asked sympathetically.

Suddenly he grinned and began strumming an imaginary guitar, singing as he strummed, "It won't be long, it won't be long. . . ."

Janie stared at him. He was looking at her expectantly, waiting for her to catch on. She dimly recalled a Beatles song he occasionally played, "It Won't Be Long." He must have been quoting from the lyrics. Now he was waiting for a comeback from her. She could barely recall all the verses to "Born to Run," which Peter considered a strong contender for the national anthem!

Maybe anything Beatles-y would do. "Help!" she said feebly. It was the best she could come up with on short notice.

Apparently it was good enough. "That's my Janie," Peter said. He reached up to tousle her hair, the way he had when she was at the station, but the French braid baffled him. "Hey," he continued, "how about coming back to KND? We really need you, kid. You kept that crazy operation on an even keel. Maybe you'd like me to teach you the board, so you could do your own show. It's a real kick, you know? What do you say?"

She gave him the same answer she had the last time he asked. But this time it was true. "I'm sorry, Peter. I just don't have the time."

"Oh." He nodded slowly. "Right. Well, just remember, the job's open."

"I will. Thanks." It made Janie ache to see the open disappointment on Peter's face. She turned away, just as Chris, sitting across the table, looked up. "Hi," she said.

"Hi," said Chris. She nodded toward the shopping bag. "Is that —"

"Oh, crumbs!" Janie interrupted. "I should have done it first thing! Here." She took the bag to the far end of the table. Chris and Phoebe followed her eagerly. She watched their faces as they opened the boxes; she saw puzzlement followed by disappointment. "What's wrong?" she said anxiously.

"I thought we were getting dresses like yours," Phoebe said. "This isn't even the right color. I don't get it."

Janie took a deep breath. "A dress like mine wouldn't do for either of you. You've got completely different figures and coloring than me."

"Yes, but —"

Janie kept talking. "My friend designed your dresses to do for you what mine does for me, to make the most of my good points and hide the bad ones. If you don't want them, you don't have

112

to take them. But give them a chance before you say no."

"Well. . . ." Chris exchanged a glance with Phoebe. "You know, Pheeb," she said, "that green is going to be gorgeous with your hair."

"Hmmm, maybe. . . . That blue is exactly the shade of your eyes. I bet it'll look awesome on you."

Some private sign passed between them. The two girls unfolded their dresses and held them up. Once again their faces fell. Janie knew why. The dresses looked plain and straight, but so had her wonderful dress when she first saw it. She knew what to do.

"Come on," she said, taking their elbows, "we're going to the girls' room. Don't say a word before you've seen them on."

They looked doubtful, but they went.

Chris's dress reflected both her classic good looks and her slightly conservative nature. The square neck, fitted waist, and slightly flared skirt were familiar; but little touches — the sleeves that ended in wide rolled cuffs just above the elbow, the subtly scalloped hem of the skirt — made it new at the same time.

For Phoebe, Henry had been more flamboyant. The dress was in two pieces. The skirt was made to hang perfectly straight from the hips to just above the knee. The top was widest at the shoulders, then narrowed evenly to the hips, creating a triangular silhouette that was echoed by the wide, deep vee of the neckline.

Janie helped the two girls into their new dresses, zipped them up, and made the delicate adjust-

113

ments that let the dresses fall as they were meant to. Both were nearly perfect fits.

Within moments, both girls had forgotten their doubts. They were happy to settle their accounts with Janie, and Chris even asked if she could order another dress when she had money again.

The number of girls who came into the bathroom while they were there astonished Janie. Even more astonishing was the number who paused to watch the try-ons, make comments, and ask questions. Many of them wanted to know which boutique they had come from.

By the time she returned to the lunchroom, Janie had received more orders for dresses. With each girl, she took down measurements and notes on coloring, then asked about favorite shades, hobbies, and interests. She knew that Henry would ask her, and she didn't want to be forced to say she didn't know.

One of the orders was from Sasha Jenkins. Janie could easily imagine the sort of dress Henry would create to suit her dreamy looks. She was also relieved to discover that she was no longer uncomfortable around Sasha. She couldn't imagine she had ever felt threatened by someone so obviously sweet and friendly. She wanted to find out how things were going at the newspaper, but Sasha left quickly after giving Janie the information for her order. She seemed very uncomfortable around Phoebe and Chris, which Janie thought was odd, since she knew the three were great friends.

Before going back to the table, Phoebe took Janie aside. "Have you heard about the fashion show next week?" she asked. Janie shook her head.

"It's going to be a mixture of loans from stores and student designs," she explained, "and I'm trying to line up participants. Would you be willing to model that wonderful tan dress of yours? I'm going to ask Chris to model hers, too. Do you think your friend would mind? Who is she, anyway?"

Janie had been getting ready for this question for days. "She doesn't want anybody to know her name," she said. "She has family problems."

"Oh. Okay, well, what if we call her the Masked Designer? Maybe Peter can dig up a tape of the William Tell Overture." Janie looked blank. "You know, the Lone Ranger theme: Da da dum, da da dum, da da dum dum dum."

Janie laughed. A mask wouldn't do much to disguise someone as tall as Henry!

"You will be in the show, won't you?" Phoebe said anxiously.

Janie nodded, but privately she was shaking her head in wonder. She, Janie Barstow, former total loser of the junior class, was being urged to appear as a model in a school fashion show! It was so crazy that it had to be true!

"Great," Phoebe said, but then she sighed. "If only I could get the guys to agree to model that easily. I have eight or ten fantastic outfits promised for the show, and practically no guys to wear them. They want to see the show, all right, but they won't take part. I guess they're scared of what it might do to their reputations."

"Why not make it a status thing to appear?"

Janie suggested. It felt very daring to offer advice to someone like Phoebe Hall, but instead of looking offended, Phoebe nodded slowly.

"Good idea," she said. "But how?"

Janie remembered what Henry had said about athletics and prestige. "Why not make it an all-star cast? You know, select one player from every sport at Kennedy and ask him. That way, it'll be an honor to be in the show. I bet no one turns you down then."

Phoebe narrowed her eyes in concentration. "You know, Janie," she finally said, "I think you've hit on it. Sure, we'll tie it in to sports. And we've already got Ted for football." She looked around in growing excitement. "Where's Woody? I've got to run this by him fast. Hey, listen, Janie, thanks for the idea. And thank your friend for my beautiful new dress!"

Chapter
11

Sasha walked briskly down the hall carrying a steno pad. She was trying to look like the picture of self-confidence and efficiency, but she felt like a heel. She hadn't dared to tell Phoebe and Chris, or anyone else, about Laurie Bennington's accusations. She was afraid they would think she was an idiot for even listening to Laurie. She was even more afraid that Laurie's version of the facts might turn out to be true. If that happened, she was going to have to write it up for *The Red and the Gold*. As a responsible journalist, her father had once told her, she could be merciful to enemies and strangers, but she could not spare her friends.

The lunchroom was nearly empty. The only one left at the crowd's table was Peter, who was listening to a tape and moodily drawing in spilt milk with a plastic stirrer. Sasha felt sorry for him. She could barely imagine how aimless she would feel if the newspaper shut down for several weeks.

Sasha tapped Peter's shoulder. He looked around and slid the earphones down onto his neck. "Have you seen Brad around?" she asked.

Peter looked up and down the table and seemed surprised that it was empty. "He *was* here," he replied, "but he's gone."

Thanks a load, Sasha thought.

"He had to do something for student government," Peter added. "Some paperwork. Try the office."

"Thanks," Sasha said, but Peter had already repositioned his earphones and touched the volume wheel of the tape player.

The door of the student council office was ajar. She tapped on it and looked around the edge. Brad's tweed jacket was on the coatrack, on a hanger. He was sitting at one end of the folding table that served as a desk, with a folder of papers in one hand and ballpoint in the other. His collar was open and the sleeves of his blue and white striped shirt were rolled halfway up his forearms. He looked harassed.

"Brad?" Sasha said. "Do you have a couple of minutes?"

"Sure," he replied, "provided you really mean a couple of minutes. I have to go over every club's budget request for the spring in time to present them to council this Thursday. The request from *The Red and the Gold* is late, by the way. Don't miss the deadline."

"We won't. Chuck and I are getting together tomorrow before school to work it out. I'll have it on your desk by noon."

"Good. Thanks for letting me know." He glanced down at the papers in his hand.

"Don't mention it," Sasha said, sitting down on a corner of the table. "But that wasn't what I wanted to talk to you about."

"Oh? What, then?"

"I wanted to talk to you about the fashion show."

"Yeah, it's just a week from tomorrow. Are you upset that the paper wasn't told sooner? I'm sorry. The truth is, we didn't get the final green light until late last week. I thought its appeal might be too limited, that most of the student body didn't care one way or another about fashion, but the organizers changed my mind."

"Organizers?" Sasha said in a neutral tone.

"I guess I should say organizer," Brad remarked, tossing his pen on the table top. "Woody dreamed it up and pushed it through. I see he's taken Phoebe in as a partner now."

A trace of bitterness crept into his voice. He obviously still put some of the blame on Woody for the fact that Phoebe had broken off their relationship. Woody had enticed her to take part in the Kennedy Follies. That had caused the first deep disagreement between Brad and Phoebe, and had pushed Phoebe toward Griffin Neal. Since then, Brad had fallen in love with Brenda, and he and Phoebe were beginning to act like friends again, so perhaps it was all for the best. But he still wasn't especially fond of Woody.

"Was the idea for the show his originally, or did he get it somewhere else?"

Brad shrugged. "I guess it was his; he never

said otherwise. He did mention brainstorming with some other students, trying to think up new projects, but I don't know if this was one of them or not."

"So you put him in charge, because you believed that it was his idea. Is that right?"

Brad sat up and looked hard at Sasha. His politician's instinct began to take control. "*I* didn't put him in charge," he said carefully. "All I did was agree to have student government sponsor something he was already organizing. The question of whose idea it was didn't even come up. He brought the idea to me and persuaded me it was a good one, so I okayed it. Come on, Sasha. These aren't the questions you usually ask about a student council event."

It was Sasha's turn to choose her words carefully. "I've been told a very different account of the beginnings of the show. Someone told me the idea was stolen from its originator and given to Woody because of cliques. I'm trying to find out what really happened."

Brad's expression hardened. "As far as I'm concerned," he said in steely tones, "that's ridiculous. I didn't take the idea away from anyone, and I don't know that anyone else did. It's not such a fantastically original idea anyway, you know. It may be a first for Kennedy, but some high schools do it every year, or even two or three times a year."

He reached for his pen and papers. "I don't know if that helps, but it's the best I can do. I've told you what my part was. Anything else you want to know, you'll have to find somebody else to ask."

Sasha knew the sound of a slamming door, and that was what she heard in his voice. "Okay, thanks," she said, standing up. "If I think of any other questions, I'll come back later."

As Sasha entered *The Red and the Gold* office, a familiar voice said, "Hiya, Jenkins, how's my favorite little fox?"

She shied away as she felt his breath on the back of her neck. "Listen, Marquette," she began, "how many times do I have to tell you —" She broke off when she realized that someone else was in the room. Laurie was sitting in her chair, idly examining the papers on her desk.

"Hello, Sasha," Laurie said silkily. "I came by to see if I could give you any more help about the fashion show. I was surprised that there wasn't anything in last week's paper."

Sasha stalked over and stood, hands on hips, next to her chair. Laurie got the message and moved to another seat. "I'm still checking it out."

"I'm sure you are. You're so incredibly responsible. I'd hate to try to get you to sit on a story that bothered me; you'd never go along with that, would you? Not even if I was your best friend." Laurie was wearing a necklace of black and gold beads with a large fake ruby pendant. She twisted it between her fingers as she spoke. "There isn't much time. The next issue of the paper is the last one before their so-called fashion show."

"I'm working on it." She was tempted to leave it there, but her sense of duty wouldn't let her. "You could answer one or two questions, though. You said that somebody stole the idea from you. How did they do that?"

"I'm afraid I'm too naive and trusting," Laurie said, lounging back in her chair and making a wide gesture with her arm. Marquette, standing behind her, leaned forward and licked his lips. "You see," she went on, "I needed advice about lighting and things like that, so I went to Woody Webster and asked for help."

"That clown," Marquette growled. "I'll wipe the grin off his face for him!"

"Be quiet, John. I thought Woody's manner seemed . . . well, odd. But he's usually a little peculiar, isn't he? The next thing, I heard that *he* was organizing a fashion show, he and his *friend*, Phoebe Hall. I went to him again, to find out what was going on, but he pretended that he didn't know what I was talking about. That's when I decided I'd better talk to you."

Sasha beat the edge of the desk with her pencil. "Was there anyone else around when you told Woody about your idea?"

"No, just the two of us."

"Hmm. Then if he says he had the idea first, it comes down to a matter of your word against his, doesn't it? I'm sorry, Laurie, but there's not much I can do in a situation like that."

"But what if I have a witness?"

"I thought you just said there weren't any?"

"Oh, not to my talk with Woody," Laurie said

122

impatiently. "But someone who can testify that I had the idea first. Here, John!"

Sasha blinked and hid a smile. From Laurie's tone speaking to the hulking wrestler, Sasha expected her to say "Sit" or "Catch!" next.

"John, tell Sasha about our talk last week."

"Uh, sure, Laurie. Well, foxette, Laurie here came over to me and told me she was putting on a fashion show and wanted to borrow some stuff from my cousin, who owns Superjock. I told her I could arrange it and she said okay. Right, Laurie?"

"Right, John. Well, Sasha? That's your evidence."

"John," Sasha said, "what day did you have this conversation?"

"What day?" he repeated, and furrowed his brow. Sasha imagined that he was mentally reciting the days of the week. "I don't know, Wednesday or Thursday, I guess."

Laurie clearly understood the importance of the question. "It was Wednesday," she said quickly, "right, John?"

"Sure, if you say so."

"I see." Sasha jotted some notes on her steno pad, then said, "Well, thanks for coming by. If I need anything more, I'll come look for you."

Laurie stood up, adjusted her blouse to expose a shapely, well-tanned shoulder, and said, "You're a doll. Oh, and I reminded my father about that book program, and he's *very* interested. We'll have to talk more after all this awful business is finished."

"See ya, little fox," John added. "I bet you can't sleep from thinking about Friday night, right? Huh, huh, huh!"

Sasha planned to find Woody after school to ask him about Laurie's allegations, but he found her first. He came up to her at her locker and said, "Hey, Sash, I want to brief you on the fashion show. You have a few minutes?"

"Sure." She led the way to the newspaper office.

"The show is next Tuesday, at three-thirty," he said as soon as they were seated. "In the Little Theater. Admission free. All the models are Kennedy students, and the fashions will include — you're not taking any notes. Are you planning to memorize all this stuff?"

"No, I'll get it down in a minute. Can I ask you a couple of questions first?" She was finding this very hard. Woody was such a sweetheart, and such a good friend. And she was about to accuse him of doing something underhanded.

"Okay, shoot."

"Where did the idea come from to do this fashion show?"

He leaned back and tucked his thumbs in his red suspenders. "Gee, I don't know. Some of us were talking about how dull it gets this time of year, and how we ought to do something interesting and fun. I tried to think of something that would involve lots of people, like the Follies, but fresher, and the idea hit me for a fashion show."

"When was this?"

He shrugged. "Last week some time. Why?"

She ignored his question. "What role did Laurie Bennington have at that point?"

He snickered. "What role? The Dragon Lady, I guess, or maybe Medusa. She'd be pretty good in either one."

"What I mean is, how did she contribute to the project?"

"She didn't." He paused, then added, "Well, to be fair about it, she did want to. She must have heard me talking to somebody about the idea, because she came up to me in the hall and offered to help. She said she knew how to get Superjock, the store in Georgetown, to participate in the show."

"What did you say?"

"I said go ahead. Why not? Oh, and she thought she should be the one to pick all the models. Can you believe it? She said that it was her right as student activities officer and that the job required a feminine viewpoint. I wanted to tell her what to do with her feminine viewpoint, but I made nice. I said I'd let her know, then just sort of forgot."

Sasha was starting to feel more like a trial lawyer than an interviewer, but she was determined to find out what had really happened. "Did Laurie have any other involvement in planning the fashion show?"

"Who cares?" Woody replied. "I sure don't." But when Sasha sat silently waiting, he added, "Yeah. She came to me a day or two later and wanted to model some European designer outfit of hers. She got really mad when I turned her down."

"Why did you do that?"

He shrugged again. "Policy. Talking it over with people, I saw that we had to keep it to stuff from stores or from student designers. Otherwise everybody would want to show off his best threads and there'd be a lot of hurt feelings. The idea of the show is to cheer things up, not make them worse."

Sasha's pencil was drumming out a military beat on the tabletop. "What you're saying, then, is that Laurie heard you mention the idea of the show and offered to take part in it? But the original idea was yours?"

"Sure. It's not *that* original, but we've never done it at Kennedy as far as I know. Sasha, what's going on? Why all the questions?"

She chewed on her lower lip and tried to decide what to do. "According to Laurie," she said at last, "the idea of doing a fashion show came from her. You then took it over and froze her out."

"That's ridiculous!" Wood roared. He didn't look quite so much like a teddy bear as usual. "That scheming so and so, she's just mad because I wouldn't let her take it over! Well, that does it. I was planning to ask Phoebe to let her model one of the outfits from Rezato, but she just blew it. The only way she'll get into my show now is through the front door, with the rest of the audience!"

Sasha waited for him to cool off a little before asking, "Can you prove that you had the idea first?"

"No, of course not! Can she prove I didn't?"

"Then it's a question of your word against hers.

Oh, Woody, I'm just trying to be a fair, responsible journalist."

"Yeah? Well, any fair, responsible person who knows Laurie Bennington and knows me will know who to believe. Right, Sasha?"

But Sasha was shuffling through some of the papers on her desk and didn't hear the question.

Chapter
12

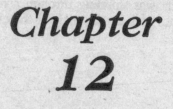

Henry was waiting near the main entrance after school. "What happened?" he demanded as soon as Janie was in hearing range. "Did they like them?"

"Well," she replied deliberately, "they were expecting something like what they'd seen me wearing, so they were a little disappointed at first."

"They were?" His long sensitive face seemed to droop.

"Uh-huh, at first. But then I explained and made them try them on. And after a while they decided that the dresses you made for them. . . ." She paused provocatively.

"What? Didn't fit? Looked ugly? *What?*"

The teasing had gone far enough. "No, silly, they decided that they were *fabulous!*" She gave him a quick hug before adding, "And you know what else? By the end of the day, I got dress

128

orders from six more girls. Six! What do you say to that?"

He didn't say anything. He looked stunned.

"And you know what else, Mr. Henry Braverman, fashion designer? The school is putting on a *Vogue/GQ* fashion show next week, and one of your designs will appear in it, modeled by none other than yours truly, Janie Barstow. *Now* what do you say?"

He looked deep into her eyes, searching for some sign that she was kidding him. Then he put back his head, opened his mouth, and let out a whoop that threatened to rattle the glass in the doors. Janie had to shake her head to get her ears working properly again.

"You really mean it, don't you? You're not joking!" Henry looked ready to let out another whoop, but Janie reached up and covered his mouth with her hand. He rolled his eyes at her. Then he took a deep breath, exhaled slowly, and said, "You're fantastic. It's all fantastic. I just can't believe it. A fashion show? And six new orders? It's incredible!"

"Incredible but true," Janie teased in a deep, spooky voice.

"Boy," Henry continued, "I've got a ton of work to do. Hey, did you get the money for the two dresses? Let's go sit down somewhere. You can tell me all about these six new girls; then I'll take the money over to Fabric Mart, buy what I'll need, and meet you at your place later."

Henry worked steadily through that entire evening. Janie's mom finally told him to go home after the eleven o'clock news ended. The same thing happened the next evening. On both nights he took home pieces that needed hand-finishing and brought them back finished the next day.

Ever since her family moved to Rose Hill, the basement rec room had been Janie's private retreat, where she went to read her fantasy novels and forget her troubles for a little while. Now it was starting to look like a busy and eccentric garment factory. Lengths of fabric in varied colors waited in neat stacks on one of the bookshelves, while scraps and remnants were slowly filling a wicker laundry basket. Paper patterns and cut-out parts of dresses were piled on the back of the old sofa. The ironing board was set up in one corner near an outlet, and in another corner, atop an old folding picnic table, was a cutting board marked off in inch squares.

Most of the new dresses were going to be variations on earlier designs, different only in color and details. For Sasha, however, Henry created an entirely new design. As Janie had expected, it was much more romantic and old-fashioned than his other dresses. It was also the one he decided to concentrate on finishing first. By the time he was sent home on Tuesday, he had the pieces of the pattern drawn and cut, ready for pinning and adjusting.

That step was going to have to wait, though. Wednesday was the day of Janie's appointment with the hair stylist. She couldn't remember when she had last been so nervous. All during the ride to the mall Henry kept reassuring her. He knew exactly what he was doing, he said, and she was going to love the results. Maybe so, she thought to herself, but if he was so sure of himself, why did he keep having to clear his throat?

The hair salon looked terrifyingly slick, the kind of place Janie wouldn't have dreamed of entering a month earlier. That didn't seem to bother Henry. He walked right in and asked to see the head stylist. In his notebook he had a page of sketches showing how he wanted Janie's hair to look from different angles. While an assistant gave her a shampoo, he and the stylist had a quiet conversation on the other side of the room. They kept glancing from her to the sketchpad and back to her. Janie's nervousness began to slide into fright. When at last the stylist walked toward her with a comb and scissors, she closed her eyes and refused to look in the mirror until he was finished with her.

She knew it was a cliché, but Janie felt as if she was looking at a stranger when she finally looked at herself. The limp bangs and long strands were gone. Now her hair came down no farther than the bottoms of her ears, and in soft, feathery layers.

Henry was standing next to Janie, smiling at her reflection. She returned the smile. She loved what the new hairstyle did for her. Its fluffiness made a wonderful frame for her facial structure, both highlighting and softening it. And her neck, so startlingly exposed, looked as long and graceful as the neck of a swan.

Janie wondered apprehensively what would happen when she went home. To her surprise, her mother loved her new haircut from the moment she walked in the door. She said so, too, so often that Janie began to be embarrassed by the attention.

"I'm just so happy to see you taking more of an interest in your appearance," her mother said during dinner. "It's not the sort of style I ever would have thought of, but it's amazingly becoming. How on earth did you decide to do it that way?"

"I don't know," Janie mumbled. "Henry gave me some advice."

"That boy has his head screwed on straight," Janie's father declared. "And as for you, sweetheart, you look quite grown up and very attractive." He punctuated his sentence with a wink.

"Ouch!" Mrs. Barstow suddenly said, and put her fingertip in her mouth. She and Janie were laying out the pattern for Sasha's dress and pinning it to the material, ready for Henry to do the delicate job of cutting. The hardest part was putting the pin through both the tissue pattern and the material without sticking it into either the cutting board or a finger.

Janie reached for the box of bandages. She was wearing two of them herself. The pinpricks didn't hurt for more than a minute, but they couldn't risk getting even a tiny bloodstain on the material. "You know," Mrs. Barstow said as she wrapped the plastic strip around her finger, "I'm sure there's a way of getting all four cuff pieces out of that one area. But I've been shifting them and shifting them, and I simply can't find it."

"Don't worry about it," Henry said. "I bought

plenty of this material. Just pin them wherever you can."

"Now, now, Henry," Mrs. Barstow replied, "you may get away with that attitude today when you're making your dresses one by one, but what about the day when you're making a dozen? Or even more? If we can fit the pattern more tightly on the fabric, we may save as much as half a yard of wasted material. That's a good deal of your potential profit that you might simply throw away instead! No, take it from me, Henry, if you're going to have the success you deserve, you'll have to be more careful."

"Thanks, Mrs. B., I'll do that," said Henry cheerfully.

Janie smiled to herself. Her mom was beginning to boss Henry around almost as much as she did Janie. But watching it happen to someone else was teaching Janie a few things. It was her mother's way of saying, I'm concerned for you, I care.

Janie learned just as important a lesson from seeing how Henry treated her mom's constant suggestions. Unlike Janie, he didn't get resentful or rebellious, because he didn't feel any force hidden behind the advice. Sure, she was saying, Do it my way, but there wasn't any Or else! at the end of the sentence. Advice was not necessarily the same thing as orders. It was simply advice, which he listened to, and then felt completely free to take or ignore.

At nine-thirty they took a break. Mrs. Barstow went upstairs to toast some muffins and make cocoa. Henry uncurled his lanky frame from the seat by the sewing machine and joined Janie in a long, luxurious stretch and yawn. Then he took her arm and sat her down on the sofa.

"There's something I want to show you," he said mysteriously. "I've been saving it all day."

He brought his large sketchpad over and sat down next to her. As he flipped through the pages, she recognized details from Chris's and Phoebe's dresses, from her own dress, and from Sasha's, as well as from designs she hadn't yet seen. Then he reached the page he was looking for and stopped.

It took some study to understand the drawing. In many ways it was the most radical design he had shown her yet. The body of the dress was pearl gray, but a broad panel of raspberry began at the right shoulder, slashed diagonally down to the left hip, then reversed course to end at the hemline, which dipped two inches lower there than on the left. The left shoulder was bare.

The raspberry panel looked almost like a sash. Yet Janie could see that it was structurally important, not mere decoration. It accentuated the vertical at the same time it drew attention to the curves that broke the vertical. It announced both I am tall and slender and I am female, without allowing either message to obscure the other.

"Henry, it's just outrageous," she exclaimed.

"Do you really like it?" There was an unusual anxiety in his voice.

"Like it! I think it's wonderful!"

"Good. Because that's the dress you're going to wear on Tuesday, in the fashion show."

Her mouth dropped open. Her, wear that? In

public? on a stage? The idea was impossible. It was like asking the guys behind the counter at a sub shop to cook a formal dinner for the White House!

"Oh, no," she said. "Uh-uh. No way. I'd just die. Besides, a dress like that deserves a real model, someone who'll make people appreciate it."

"You," he said flatly. "I designed it for you. Either you wear it or nobody does."

"Henry, I can't. I'd love to, but I'm just not the kind of girl who can wear something like that. It's too . . . oh, I don't know what, but people would laugh. They wouldn't see how great your dress is, they'd just see me!"

"You can be whatever kind of girl you really want to be. Look at the drawing. Does it make you want to laugh?"

"No, of course not."

"Fine! Because that's you, wearing my dress! Didn't it look familiar?"

She looked again. It was true: The hairstyle in the drawing was her own, and so were the contours of the body. The face was extremely stylized, just a line or two for the features, but even there she began to see a resemblance. Could she, Janie Barstow, really look like that?

Henry saw her wavering and pressed his attack. "You don't have to make up your mind now," he said. "As soon as I get Sasha's dress out of the way, I'm starting on this one. When it's done, put it on, go to the mirror, and then decide."

"But Henry, what if I say no? All that wasted work!"

He shrugged his shoulders. "It uses some ideas

135

and techniques I've never tried before, so the work wouldn't really be wasted." Then, hearing voices from the top of the stairs, he shut the sketchbook.

Mrs. Barstow appeared with a plate of blueberry muffins, followed by Janie's father carrying a tray with mugs of hot cocoa. He set it down, looked around the room, and said to Henry, "So this is the new enterprise, is it?"

"Yes, sir," Henry said.

Janie looked at him in surprise. Whenever her dad was around, Henry's whole personality seemed to shut down. All his interests, intelligence, and quick perceptions disappeared.

In fact, if Janie had met Henry when he was like this, she probably would have put him down as one of the most boring guys she had ever met. Yet she knew that wasn't what he was really like.

"I wanted to see for myself," Mr. Barstow continued in a hearty tone. "In banking, we get to be in at the start of lots of operations, you know. As soon as a new business gets a bit successful, it comes to the bank for the money to expand. But it's not often that we can watch the process under our own roofs, is it?"

He gave a chuckle, and seemed to expect Henry to join him. But all Henry said was, "No, sir," in that same voice.

"Tell me, son. . . ."

Henry flinched.

". . . have you thought about where to take this? What are your plans?"

Faced with a question that couldn't be answered yes or no, Henry squared his shoulders, took an audible breath, and said, "College, I guess. Maybe design school in New York. Some-day I'd like a career as a designer."

"Someday?" Mr. Barstow echoed. "It appears to me that you're heading that way right now. I'm no expert on the fashion industry, mind you, but I think you're on to something here. Your growth rate so far is in the neighborhood of three hundred percent a week!" He chuckled again, and this time Henry did join in.

"Don't think small," Mr. Barstow concluded. "And don't sell yourself short. With some expert advice and a little backing, you just might be able to get a headstart on that career of yours."

"Do you really think so, sir?" Henry asked eagerly.

"I just said it. And if you'd like to talk with me some more about your business plans, I'd be happy to. You know where to find me," he added with a twinkle. "Right up the stairs from your sweatshop!"

Later, when he and Janie were alone, Henry said, "Your dad meant what he said, didn't he? About wanting to help me get started?"

"Sure," Janie replied. "He's very impressed with you. He thinks most of our generation 'lack the spirit of enterprise that made America great.' " She gave the words a wry twist, as if she had heard them too often to take them very seriously.

"And he doesn't think I'm weird for wanting to design clothes?"

"Nope. Why should he? There are dozens of very successful designers, and probably a lot more who are pretty successful. Are they weird? Dad

137

likes people who are involved in what they're doing and who care about doing it well."

They worked in silence for almost an hour more. Then Mrs. Barstow called from upstairs, "Okay, you two, time's up. School tomorrow, you know."

Janie stopped on the first step and turned around. "Henry," she said softly. "About my new dress, I don't know if I'll have the guts to wear it in the show. But I want you to know that I think it's beautiful. Thank you."

"You're welcome." His voice filled the formula with meaning. He gazed solemnly into her eyes and for an instant his body began to sway toward hers. Then, just as she was closing her eyes and imagining how his lips would feel on hers, he blinked, gulped, and said, "Er, well, good-night, Janie."

Janie walked him to the back door, waved, and closed the door. Then she gave the table leg a solid kick and said, "Oh, *rats!*"

Chapter *13*

When Phoebe emerged from history class on Friday morning, she saw the new issue of *The Red and the Gold* in a stack outside the classroom. She took a copy and glanced at the front page. It took her a moment to find, but there it was, in the lower left-hand corner: VOGUE/GQ HITS KENNEDY TUESDAY. Good. The show was taking place on such short notice that it needed all the publicity it could get.

She would have liked a bigger headline, maybe even a banner across the top, but editors had their own peculiar ideas of what was important. With luck and the help of a poster campaign on Monday and Tuesday, the show might even draw a big enough crowd to justify all the hassles she had been dealing with. She tucked the newspaper in her looseleaf and went to her next class.

Lunch was a yogurt and a soda in the student council office. She had a dozen telephone calls to make, memos to write to the sound and light crews, and a combined planning session and rehearsal to arrange for that afternoon. Not to mention creating an order for the show, and making sure that somebody picked up the posters. There had been a time when she envied her friends — Brad, and Sasha, and Peter — who were deeply involved in school activities. Now she was starting to think that she had been the lucky one and had never known it.

By the time she finished her chores, she had ten minutes and a half can of warm soda left. She found the newspaper, tilted her chair back on two legs, and prepared to enjoy some moments of calm before she had to go to class. But as she read the story about the fashion show, she began to frown.

All the necessary information was there: who, what, when, where. But there was something disturbing about the article. It wasn't just the lack of enthusiasm. The reader was left with a slight distaste, a vague feeling that there was something wrong with the whole project. Phoebe was also a little hurt to see that neither her name nor Woody's was mentioned anywhere in the article. She wasn't in it for the glory, but with the amount of work she was doing, it would have been nice to get some credit.

On her way to class, she noticed the door to the newspaper office was ajar. She pushed it wider and looked in. Sasha was at her desk, her chin cupped in her hands, staring down at a copy of the paper. She looked very unhappy. Phoebe was tempted not to bother her, but before she could retreat, Sasha looked up and saw her. "Hello," she said in a dismal voice.

"Hi, Sash. Are you okay?"

"Sure." She made a weak attempt at a smile. "I need to cut down on sugar, that's all. Too much sugar puts you on an emotional roller coaster."

"Oh." As usual, Phoebe let her friend's comment on nutrition go by. "Hey, listen, I've got to get to class, but I wanted to ask you about the story about the *Vogue/GQ* show."

To her surprise, Sasha's face started to turn bright pink. "What about it?" she said.

"Well. . . ." Phoebe considered letting it slide. Why upset her friend over something so trivial? On the other hand, why should Sasha get upset over something so trivial? "It's not really important," she said cautiously, "and maybe you didn't have room, but I sort of wondered why you didn't mention Woody or me. The paper usually names the students who are running a project, doesn't it?"

"Sometimes we do and sometimes we don't." She spoke as if she were testifying before a Congressional committee. "It's purely a matter of our editorial judgment."

"Oh, sure," Phoebe said. What she wanted to say was, Huh?

Sasha pushed herself up out of her chair and leaned across the desk toward Phoebe. "*The Red and the Gold* is an independent newspaper. It's my job to report the news as objectively as possible. That means I have to report my stories as though you and Woody are just two ordinary people — not two of my best friends who deserve special favors or consideration."

"But, Sasha," Phoebe said. "All I asked was why the paper is ignoring all the work Woody and I are doing for the *Vogue/GQ* show. So what if we're friends of yours? Is that any reason to act as if we don't exist?"

Sasha looked away in confusion. "I'm sorry, Phoebe," she said. "I'm very busy right now with a story. Can we talk later?"

At that moment, the buzzer sounded in the hall. Phoebe was already late for class. She wanted to stay, to find out what was bothering Sasha. But Sasha didn't seem to want her to stay, anyway. "Well, look," Phoebe said awkwardly, "I'll catch you later."

Sasha didn't answer. After another long, uncertain pause, Phoebe left the room.

As the sound of Phoebe's footsteps faded, Sasha started rubbing her forehead and temples. Maybe she lacked the strength of character to be a real journalist. She hadn't been aware, when she wrote the article about the *Vogue/GQ* show, that she wasn't mentioning Woody and Phoebe. But now, she realized that it had not been an accident. By leaving them out, she was somehow making up for not printing anything about Laurie's accusations.

That had been a deliberate decision. She had had a long, intense debate with herself. If what Laurie had told her was accurate, it was an important story. It said a great deal about the way student government was conducted, and how it favored those who had friends in positions of power. It was exactly the kind of story a self-respecting journalist had to write and a responsible newspaper had to print.

But she didn't believe Laurie's account was accurate. Woody had explained the facts at least as persuasively as Laurie had. Brad's statements didn't support or contradict either of them. And when she took a close look at what John Marquette had said, it seemed to fit just as well with either account. In the end, Sasha decided that there simply wasn't enough evidence to justify printing a story like that. The fact that she liked Woody, and Phoebe was her closest friend, had not influenced her at all.

Or had it? She couldn't really be sure. Maybe her friends' dislike of Laurie and her bias in favor of her friends had affected the way she listened, evaluated, and reached a decision.

Laurie certainly thought it had. She had told Sasha so, several times, very loudly, not an hour earlier. The memory of that exchange still flamed in Sasha's mind. Laurie had flung the door open and stalked into the office, waving a copy of *The Red and the Gold*. She was wearing a dropped-waist minidress in neon orange with acid green anklets and a matching scarf knotted at the neck, but her outfit was pale compared to the expression on her face.

"You've really disappointed me, Sasha," she began.

Sasha clasped her hands together to keep them from trembling. "I don't know what you're talking

143

about, Laurie," she said as calmly as she could.

"Oh, yes you do!" Laurie made no effort to control her own anger. "Where's the story? Where's your exposé of Woody Webster, and Phoebe Hall, and Brad Davidson, and the way they stole the fashion show idea from me? Were you too afraid to get on the wrong side of your friends? Don't you realize that they're just using you?"

Sasha worked on keeping her breathing slow and even. "I looked into your story," she began. "Woody told me a completely different account of what happened. Since it came down to your unsupported word against his, I couldn't use the story. And I don't think I like your tone."

"My tone!" Laurie screeched. She clenched her hands, digging her long, crimson nails into her palms. "I'll give you tone, Sasha Jenkins! And what do you mean, unsupported? Didn't John confirm what I told you? Are you calling him a liar? Don't forget that his cousin is one of the biggest advertisers in your little rag!"

Sasha had been goaded with this stick once too often. "John Marquette and his cousin can both take a running jump off the Key Bridge," she exclaimed. "This newspaper can get along without them if it has to. And as for John's evidence, it didn't really confirm your story. Woody's account of what happened explains it just as well as yours, so it's still his word against yours."

"All right!" Laurie's eyes narrowed, and her voice became quieter but more menacing. "All right! I know what I'm up against. This isn't the first time your little clique has tried to get the

144

better of me. But I warn you, Sasha, I won't be silenced. Other people will learn about this. They'll find out about your unprofessional and unethical conduct. And I'll make sure they find out before student council takes up your spring budget request, too!"

Sasha thought that that was Laurie's parting shot, but at the door she turned and said, in a fake-sweet voice, "Oh, and about that TV show on books. I talked it over with my father, and he decided that he wants someone with more prestige and authority than the owner of a two-bit suburban bookstore. Sorry."

Janie glanced at her watch as she neared *The Red and the Gold* office. She was due at a planning meeting for the big fashion show in ten minutes, and she did not want to be late. Henry was meeting her outside the Little Theater and coming to the meeting, too. Not as the Masked Designer, of course; just as someone who was volunteering to help on the show.

Before going across to the theater, however, Janie was determined to give Sasha Jenkins her new dress. She had looked for Sasha in the cafeteria at lunch, but Kennedy's ace reporter must have been eating at her desk.

She still was, apparently. At least, when Janie opened the door, she was sitting at her desk eating a chocolate cupcake and drinking a soda from the vending machines outside the lunchroom.

"Hi," Janie said brightly.

"Hello," Sasha replied in a dreary voice. "You look different."

145

"I got my hair cut. Like it?"

"It's very pretty. What's the occasion?"

Janie smiled. "It was time, that's all. Oh, and the show, too. I'm going to be modeling one of my friend's dresses."

After saying this, she worried that it might sound too much like boasting. "That's why I came by," she added. "To bring you your dress. I told you the other day it would be done by Friday, and here it is!" She held up the box proudly.

Interest flared in Sasha's face. "Really? Wow, let's see! Is it more like Chris's or Phoebe's?"

"Neither one. I told you that my friend makes dresses to go with each individual personality. You're not like Phoebe or Chris, and your dress isn't like theirs. See?"

She opened the box and folded back the tissue paper. "Oh," Sasha whispered, "it's lilac. That's my favorite color. How did you know?"

Janie smiled to herself. There wasn't any magic involved. On Monday, when she took the order, one of the questions she had asked was what Sasha's favorite color was. But she wasn't going to reveal any trade secrets. All she said was, "Lift it out."

The waist was high and bound with a long, wide sash, and the full pleated skirt fell in soft folds to below the knee. The scoop neck, fitted bodice, and full sleeves completed the picture.

"It's beautiful," Sasha said.

"You have to try it on. It's the only way to know how it really looks."

"I can change right here," Sasha said. "Would

146

you watch the door for me?" A few moments later she said shyly, "How does it look?"

Janie smiled. Together with her huge brown eyes and wavy brown hair, the dress made Sasha look exactly as if she could pose for the cover of *Jane Eyre*. When she said so, Sasha gasped. "That's one of my all-time favorite books," she said. "Do I really? That's wonderful! Oh, I wish we had a big mirror in here."

"Sure," Janie chuckled. "What's a newspaper office without a big mirror?" Inwardly she marveled at the change in herself. It hadn't been long since she was terrified of even passing Sasha Jenkins in the hall, and here she was teasing her. "Come on, we'll visit the girls' room."

Sasha couldn't stop admiring the dress in the mirror. She turned to one side and the other, even turning around and trying to look over her shoulder. "It's just perfect," she repeated for the seventeenth time. "How can I ever thank you and your mysterious friend?"

Suddenly her face fell. "Oh, golly," she said in a voice of alarm. "I completely forgot!"

"What?"

"The money! I know you told me the dress would be ready today, but I guess I didn't really believe it. So I left the money at home. It's sitting in an old teapot on top of my dresser. I even thought about bringing it this morning, but I don't like to carry more than I need. I'm such an idiot!"

"Don't worry about it," Janie said soothingly. "You can pay me on Monday."

"You won't take the dress back, will you?"

Her voice, like her expression, was achingly wistful.

"Of course not. It's *your* dress."

"I could kick myself for forgetting! Listen, Janie, come back to the office and let me see what I've got in my purse. At least I can give you a deposit."

"No, no, don't bother," Janie replied. "Pay me on Monday.

But Sasha insisted. She dragged Janie back and searched through her purse, her pockets, and her knapsack. She even checked her desk drawer. The total was a five, a single, and eighty-three cents in change. She pushed it across to Janie. "Please take it," she said. "I'll feel better knowing that the dress is at least partly mine."

Janie was already late for the meeting. "Okay. But why don't you keep the change?"

Sasha shook her head. "No. I don't need it. Take it all."

Chapter
14

Phoebe looked around the gym and shook her head. "I don't like it," she said. "This place is too big. What if nobody comes?"

"They'll come," Woody said. He had spent much of the planning session arguing for a shift from the Little Theater to the gym. "It's not just that we need all these seats, either. If we put the models on a stage, it'll look like theater. If they're down here surrounded by an audience, it'll feel like a fashion show. And that's what we're after, right? What do you think, Janie?"

Janie looked at the rows of bleachers and imagined walking down between them. "This'll be a lot scarier," she replied. "There isn't any place to hide. But I think the clothes will show up better."

Woody smiled triumphantly. "Well, Pheeb-a-rebop, what do you say now?"

"Oh, all right. But it'll mean lots more work.

We'll have to put up the curtains for the dressing areas before Monday's rehearsal, then take them down and put them up again on Tuesday. And we'd better hope nobody fools with the lights between the rehearsal and the show." She opened her notebook and wrote several notes to herself.

"No problem," Woody said cheerfully. "We'll have lots of help. Henry will lend a hand. Right, Henry?"

"Sure." Janie had introduced him simply as someone who wanted to help on the show. The others had given him a friendly welcome. Thanks in part to Janie's idea of selecting sports stars, they had plenty of models, but people willing to work away from the spotlight were harder to find.

"In fact," Woody continued, "why don't we go take a look at those curtains right now. If there's a problem, I'd rather not find out about it on Monday afternoon."

Trailed by Phoebe and Henry, he started for the far end of the gym. Janie was about to follow them when Peter Lacey called to her from the sound booth. "I want to talk to you," he said. "It won't take a minute."

Curious, she clambered up the bleachers to the tiny glass-walled room. Peter was busy patching a tape deck and portable mixer into the PA system amp. "Hey, how does it look?" he said. "The fidelity will probably look sick next to a $19.95 car radio, but I'll have lots of watts to burn. I wanted to know about your music."

"My music?" Janie said blankly.

"Yeah, for Tuesday afternoon. What do you want, a march, a waltz, or disco? The others will

150

take what they get, but since we're old partners, I figured I'd ask you for a preference. I'm putting the tape together over the weekend, so I gotta know now."

The question hadn't even occurred to Janie until that moment. She thought of telling Peter to use his own taste, but then she realized that that would probably mean Springsteen. Not quite right for the occasion. "Could you find something," she said tentatively, "that sounds up-to-date but kind of mellow, like slow New Wave? Something I can walk to?"

"Hey, no problem! There's a cut from the new Posers album that might do."

"Great. Thanks, Peter."

Janie was turning to go when he added, "Are you tied up after this? I thought when I got finished here, maybe we could go get something to eat together."

Janie blinked and said, "I'm not sure. I have to check." She hesitated, then said, "By the way, what do you hear from Lisa?" Lisa Chang was the champion figure skater whom Peter had fallen in love with just before she was accepted to an Olympic training program in Colorado.

"Not much. I think they're keeping her pretty busy preparing for a big competition next month."

"Oh," Janie said, eyeing him curiously. "Well, give her my love next time you talk. I'll catch you later."

Henry was coming back to see what was keeping Janie when he saw her half-running from the gym. He lengthened his stride and caught up to her just as she reached the doors.

"Janie?" he said. She refused to look at him. "Janie, what is it?"

"Nothing," she said in a muffled voice.

"It isn't nothing," he insisted. "What's wrong?" He took her shoulders and turned her toward him. As he expected, she was on the verge of tears. "What's wrong?" he repeated.

"Peter Lacey just asked me for a date," she replied. "Tonight."

"Oh?" he said carefully. "And that upset you?"

"Of course it did! Henry, all last fall I did everything I could to get him to like me. I brought him coffee, and made him cookies, and practically ran that dumb radio station of his. And he paid less attention to me than to a new album by the Clash. I was part of the equipment."

"I'm sure he didn't —"

Janie interrupted him. "And now, just because I dress differently and cut my hair, the elusive Peter Lacey wants to take me out to dinner! But *I* haven't changed. I'm still the same girl he used to treat like a piece of furniture. Is that all that counts — *looks*? That stinks!"

Instead of speaking, Henry pulled her closer and wrapped his arms around her. Her body, tense at first, began to relax. Then she started to cry. He rubbed her back and waited until she was cried out. Then he said, "It wasn't looks that he was noticing, it was the change in you. The haircut and the clothes don't really make you look that different. Your old friends from Cincinnati would still know it was you. But you feel different about yourself. You walk and talk differently. You stand up and speak out. You've stopped trying to disappear. And that makes all the difference."

She pulled back to look up into his face. "You did it," she said softly. "You made me a different person."

He shook his head. "I just made the clothes," he said. "You made the person. But I've always thought you were beautiful." Slowly, tentatively, he bent over and kissed her. For a moment she stood very still. Then, as he began to pull away, she put her arms around his neck and pulled his lips down onto hers again.

"What should I tell Peter?" Janie murmured during a pause for breath.

"Tell him you already have a date. Tell him you're having a very special dinner with me tonight."

"Mmm," Janie replied as he pulled her close again. "I'll do that. In a little while."

Sasha wrapped her down coat more tightly around her and shivered. The heater in John Marquette's old convertible was practically roasting her left ankle and doing nothing for the rest of her. She peered out the windshield at the narrow Georgetown streets trying to decide where they were, but the rows of old townhouses all looked the same.

The snow was starting to fall more heavily. It was beautiful under the glow of the old-fashioned streetlights. She wished she could give herself up to enjoying it, but she had to devote part of her attention to the job of keeping her thigh out of

John Marquette's reach. It wasn't easy, especially when his huge hand groped for the gearshift lever.

She never should have agreed to this plan. She had been so certain that she could handle him. After all, he was a lot like a dinosaur: big as a house, with a brain the size of a pea. But now, too late, it occurred to her that going out with a dinosaur wouldn't have been a very good idea, either.

"We're almost there," Marquette shouted over the buzz of the engine. "It's a great place. Wait'll the fellows get a load of my little fox. They'll be green!"

"I'm not —" Sasha began, then shut up. There was no use in protesting. Marquette was either stubborn or stupid. Or maybe both. Whichever, she was wasting her time trying to correct him.

He suddenly spotted an empty parking place and yanked the wheel. Sasha's stomach lurched as the rear wheels slid on the slick pavement. She grabbed the armrest, but at that instant Marquette pulled the parking brake, turned off the ignition, and said, "Here we are." He reached across her and tripped the door latch. "Ladies first.

"My cousin lives in that building," he added when he joined her on the sidewalk. "It's a great pad. I stay there sometimes when I'm working late at the store. He's in New York this weekend."

Sasha didn't even look. She had no interest in John's cousin or his pad. She was interested only in getting through this ridiculous dinner and going home.

The tavern was obviously a favorite hangout for college athletes. Team photos and banners covered the walls, and a shelf behind the bar held a long row of trophies. The huge color TV was tuned to a pro basketball game. The noise and smoke made Sasha's head ache and her eyes water. Marquette led her to an empty booth near the back, jostling five or six people as he went. A couple of them spun around angrily, then turned away muttering after they saw him.

"You want a beer?" Marquette asked. When Sasha shook her head, he added, "Don't worry, foxette, I brought ID for you and me both. I always go prepared on dates."

"This isn't a date," she said. "It's an interview." She reached under the table, took his hand off her knee, and picked up her notebook. "Now, about the way the athletics department is run —"

"Later, Jenkins. We gotta order. They close the kitchen at eight. How about a rare steak sandwich and double fries?"

Sasha felt faint at the thought. "Can I get a salad?" she asked weakly.

"Huh, huh," Marquette laughed. "I guess maybe Tony can find some lettuce for you if I ask him nicely. How about a carrot, too?"

"Thanks. I like raw carrots. Is it true that the grade records of some team members have been changed to keep them eligible to play?"

The restaurant Henry and Janie entered was on the ground floor of an old house in Georgetown. As they waited for a table, Janie looked at the old brick walls warmed by candlelight and lowered her voice. "Are you sure this is okay? Won't it cost an awful lot?"

"Didn't you hear your father?" he teased. "My business is expanding three hundred percent a week. Four weeks from now I plan to buy this place!"

She giggled happily and nestled closer to him. He had kept his arm around her as they were walking from the car, and she was already missing it.

"Anyway," he added, more seriously, "this is our first date. As a matter of fact, it's my first date ever. . . ."

"Mine, too," Janie confessed. She didn't count homecoming as a date.

". . . and I want it to be an evening we can always remember."

"It will be," Janie said. Her eyes were glistening. "It will be."

A low-pitched voice broke the moment of silence that followed. "Monsieur, mademoiselle, your table is ready."

"Then at my next meet I flattened Walt Koerner. They had to scrape him off the mat with a shovel." Marquette waved his empty beer mug at the waiter as he said, "Hey, fox, you're not writing any of this down! I've got some real scoops I could give you, but you got to make me want to give them, if you know what I mean."

Sasha knew exactly what he meant. She twisted sideways to avoid a groping hand and took another gulp of her spring water. A drop of the bottled dressing that was tying her stomach in knots fell on the skirt of her new lavender dress.

As she dipped her napkin in her glass and dabbed the spot, Marquette blustered on.

"You got to give if you want to get," John repeated. "Take that clown Webster. When he wanted my cousin's store to lend stuff for his Mickey Mouse fashion show, he knew better than to ask me himself. I would have turned him down, and then I would have shoved his head between his shoulder blades for asking. But when he got Laurie to ask me nicely" — he raised his eyebrows in a grotesque caricature — "I went along, and so did my cousin."

Except for a single rapid blink, Sasha's face did not change. Nor did her voice as she asked, "Is that how Woody got you to cooperate, by asking Laurie Bennington to ask you?"

"That's what I just said, isn't it?"

So she hadn't corrupted her professional ethics. Her instinct to distrust Laurie's tale had been absolutely correct. She was so relieved by this discovery that she almost didn't notice John's hand grabbing her knee. By the time she tried to react, he had a grip on her that showed how he had become all-district wrestling champ. After a few useless tugs and twists, she began to wonder if she should make a scene. But at that moment he released her knee in order to grab — and finish in one long series of swallows — his fresh mug of beer.

While they ate their tossed salads and freshly baked rolls, Janie talked about her childhood in Ohio. She had been shy even then, though not as shy as she became after moving to Rose Hill. She spoke of picnics and vacations, lemonade in the backyard, and how much she had liked taking care of the twins when they were babies. But gradually she sensed that Henry was not really listening. She trailed off into silence.

Neither of them spoke while the waiter cleared the salad plates. But when he was gone, Janie decided that she was not going to go on like that. She had to know what was happening.

"Henry?" she said softly. He didn't react. She reached for his hand and squeezed it. "Henry, what is it? What's wrong?"

He sighed. "I just don't know what to do. When I went home to change and pick up Mom's car, I ran into my father. He's planning to come see me play next Wednesday night. He even apologized for missing my other games this season."

"Uh-oh," Janie murmured.

"What am I going to do? In less than a week, my whole life is going to go right down the tubes." He ran his hands nervously through his hair, then glanced around the restaurant and hastily put them in his lap.

"There's only one thing you can do," Janie replied. "You have to tell him the truth."

"He'll murder me! I'm not kidding, he will!"

"You have to stand up to him and make him see that you are your own person. He may not like it, but if he's any kind of man he will have to respect it."

"Sure," Henry said, "he'll respect all the little pieces he's scattered all over the neighborhood.

Janie, what kind of books have you been reading?"

"Well, maybe I sound naive or dumb," she said stubbornly, "but I still think I'm right. You've got to tell him the truth. You don't have any choice. What are you going to do, bribe the coach to let you play on the team for one game?"

"I don't know. All I know is that I don't have much time to decide. Wednesday isn't far away."

As the waiter arrived with their main dishes, Janie made another attempt to cheer Henry up. "That's true," she said, "but Tuesday is even closer. And Tuesday may change your life!"

Chapter
15

"Hey, I just remembered," Marquette said as he and Sasha walked back to the car. "You wanted to know about grade point averages and team members, right? Well, I happen to have a copy of a report the athletics department made on that. It's not supposed to be public, but I guess you could look at it, for background."

Sasha glanced over at him. His letter jacket over a thick sweater made him look even bulkier than usual, and with each beer his tiny eyes had seemed to recede farther into his head. Some instinct told her to forget the story and go straight home, but she couldn't do it. Nothing could make that awful dinner worthwhile, but she would feel like less of a fool if she had something to show for it. "Sure," she said, "I'd like to see that. Can you bring it to me on Monday?"

"No need, it's right here. I told you I keep a lot of stuff at my cousin's, didn't I? Come on."

"That's okay," Sasha said, holding back. "It can wait. I'm sort of tired."

"Hey, look," Marquette growled. "If you want to see it, you come do it right now or forget the whole thing. I'm the one who's doing you the favor, don't forget. I have to go up and get something anyway, so are you coming or not?"

Reluctantly, Sasha followed him into the building and up the stairs. His shoulders took up the entire width of the hallway. Two steps into the apartment, she realized that she had made a mistake. A big, wide couch and a huge TV and VCR were practically the only furnishings in the room. Through an open doorway she could see a king-size waterbed. She didn't see any place that John might have left an athletics department report.

"Here, let me take your coat," he said, grabbing the collar.

She held it tightly closed. "No, thanks, I'm a little chilly."

"Don't worry, little fox," he said, trying to nuzzle her neck. "I can fix that in no time. Hey, you want to watch something? My cousin has a great collection of videotapes. Sit down and I'll find a really hot one."

Sasha ducked away from him, put her back to the wall, and crossed her arms. "No, thanks. If you'll find that report, I want to go home."

He snorted and wandered into the kitchenette. When he returned, he was carrying an open bottle of vodka by the neck. "Want a drink?" He waved it in her direction. "It'll warm you up." When she shook her head, he put the bottle to his lips and took two or three gulps.

161

At this point Sasha knew she was in trouble. She should have listened to her friends' warnings about John Marquette. He was turning out to be every bit the animal they said he was. But this wasn't the time to reproach herself. She had to figure out what to do, and do it quickly.

Her parents had always told her if she got into a situation she couldn't handle, she should call them at once. "I have to call my parents," Sasha said firmly. "Where's the phone?"

"The phone?" John took another swallow from the bottle, then went behind the sofa and bent down. But instead of handing her the telephone, he unplugged it and tossed it through the doorway onto the waterbed. "The phone's in the bedroom," he said with a grotesque wink. "Come on, I'll help you get your number."

"No, thanks, I'll go find a pay phone." But even as she spoke, Sasha remembered that she had given Janie Barstow every penny she had. What was worse, her mom had mentioned at breakfast that they were going to a friend's poetry reading this evening, but hadn't mentioned the friend's name. Even if she found a telephone and borrowed the change, she wouldn't know who to call.

Marquette walked deliberately across the room and leaned one hand against the door. "Don't go, my little fox," he said in a voice thickened by the vodka. "I can give you a real good time. Come on."

In spite of his size, Marquette was fast. A hand snaked out and pulled her coat down to her elbows. "You can't have a good time all bundled up like that," he said.

Torn between fear and rage, Sasha jerked away. "Let go of me," she demanded in a rising voice, "and let me out of here! Right now!"

"Oh, no, you don't," he said, grabbing the sleeve of her dress and pulling her close to him. "Listen, Jenkins, you've been stringing me along for weeks. Well, it's time to come through!" He started to drag her toward the couch. His raw strength was astonishing.

"Let me go or I'll scream!" Near hysteria, she began to struggle wildly. He barely noticed. He even paused for a moment to swig down more vodka before tugging at her arm again.

Suddenly, with a noise that was startlingly loud, the fabric of the sleeve began to rip. It tore from the shoulder seam nearly to the elbow. Both of them stared as if the sleeve had decided to rip itself, with no human involvement at all. Then Sasha wailed, "You've ruined my new dress!" and burst into tears.

Marquette backed away. A look of nervousness, even fear, began to overwhelm his face. "Hey, I was only kidding," he mumbled. "I'll buy you another dress, okay? Just stop making so much racket. The neighbors might call the cops."

"Take me home! I want to go home!"

"Okay, okay!" He made wide motions with his hands. "I'll take you home right now. Just shut up!" He reeled into the kitchen and returned without the bottle. "Come on. I'm taking you home."

Sasha pulled her coat up over the ruined sleeve, wiped her eyes, and went out onto the stairs.

163

Marquette followed more slowly. He had trouble putting the key into lock the door, and on the first step he stumbled, and had to grab the bannister to keep from plunging headlong.

Outside, the snow was falling again, more heavily than before. Marquette cursed as he staggered off the walk into the gutter and his shoes filled with snow and slush. "Come on," he called, "get in the car!"

Sasha realized that she had tumbled from one danger into another. John would have been too drunk to drive even if the streets had been clear and dry. In this snowstorm, riding with him would be suicide.

"No," she said firmly. "You shouldn't drive. You've had too much to drink."

"Me?" He reeled over and stuck his face in hers. "Listen, foxette, I can drink twice as much, five times as much as I had tonight, and still drive better 'n you do cold sober! Now get in the car or I'm leaving you here!"

Janie and Henry walked arm in arm down the quiet street. From start to finish, the dinner had been just what Janie had hoped it would be. Not that she paid very much attention to the food. They were too busy getting to know each other better. She had even managed to get his mind off his father by asking Henry how he had become interested in design.

Henry was like her in so many ways. He was helping her to overcome her shyness; she desperately wanted to help him in some way. As long as he remained terrified of discovery by his father, he was going to go on keeping his real nature and interests hidden from almost everyone.

Janie stuck out her tongue to catch a snowflake. "I wish we could walk all the way home," she said. "The light is so strange, almost as bright as day."

"That's all the lights of the city reflecting off the snow," Henry said. "Sometimes it's so bright you can read a book by it."

"And so quiet! I feel like I ought to whisper, but even if I shouted I don't think anybody would hear. It reminds me of hiding under my down comforter during thunderstorms. That was when I was *very* little, of course," she added hastily.

"Of course," he agreed gravely. "The car's around this corner, I think."

"Wait," Janie said. "Listen! Isn't that somebody shouting?"

They both stood still and turned their heads from side to side, trying to locate the elusive sound. Suddenly Henry pointed to the right. "Over there," he said. "Sounds like trouble. Come on."

He took off, running awkwardly through the snow, with Janie right behind him. As they drew closer, they saw two people, one much bigger than the other, struggling next to a car.

"Hey," Henry shouted, "let go of her!"

"Make her let go of me!" a slurred voice replied.

"Sasha!" Janie called in astonishment. "Is that you?"

"Janie, thank goodness! But what are you doing here?"

"Well, whadayaknow," the slurred voice continued, "if it isn't Olive Oyl! Who's your friend? Does Popeye know you're sneaking around with another guy?"

Janie turned beet red. John Marquette! He had humiliated her once before but she refused to listen to his taunts again. She turned away from him and said, "Sasha, are you okay?"

"What's going on?" Henry demanded at the same time.

"I'm okay," Sasha said breathlessly. "I was supposed to interview John, for an article, but he got drunk. And now he wants to drive back to Rose Hill, but I won't let him. He's bound to get into a crash and kill somebody."

"I'm *not* drunk," Marquette roared, and lurched toward his car.

Henry grabbed his arm. "Hey, hang on," he said. "Why don't you let me drive you home? You can come get your car tomorrow when you're feeling better."

Marquette struck Henry's hand away. "You keep out of this, you and Olive Oyl both. Take the Ice Queen home if you want, I'm going by myself."

As Marquette reeled toward the car again, Henry stepped in front of him. "You're in no shape to drive, fellow. Give yourself a break and come with us."

"I'll give you a break, turkey! What do you want broken — an arm, a leg, or your stupid neck? Hey," he added, staring blearily at Henry, "I know who you are. Braverman. Right. Your old man

166

coaches football at Rose Hill. Boy, I bet he can't believe he's got you for a son!"

Henry straightened up to his full height, pulled back his right fist, and let Marquette have it right in the mouth. The burly wrestler took a surprised step backward, slipped on a patch of ice, and fell heavily to the ground where he lay, too stunned to move.

"Henry!" Janie exclaimed. "What are you doing?"

"I'm sorry," he said sheepishly. "I never did anything like that before. I guess the whole business with my father has been getting to me, and all of a sudden I couldn't take any more."

"What do we do now?" Sasha said. "Is he hurt?"

Marquette's eyes were closed, but his lips were moving. Fearing a trick, Henry went behind his head and knelt down. He could hear a tuneless voice singing, "Fight, fight for Kennedy High. . . ."

"He's okay," Henry said shortly. "I don't know how we can get him home, though."

"We can leave him here," Sasha suggested.

Janie was shocked. "In the snow? He'll freeze!"

"No, no, at his cousin's. It's right here, one flight up."

After some more debate, they woke Marquette enough to get him on his feet. Henry took one side, Janie took the other, and Sasha pushed from behind. After a struggle that would have been funny if it hadn't been so exhausting, they wrestled Marquette up to his cousin's apartment. He immediately collapsed on the sofa and started to snore.

They left him there and got in Henry's car for the trip back to Rose Hill. As they drove off, Sasha started to weep. Janie stroked her head. "Don't cry," she murmured. "It's all right now."

"No, it isn't," Sasha wailed. "He tore the sleeve on my beautiful new dress, the one your friend made for me. The first time I wore it, and it's ruined!"

By the light of a passing streetlamp, Janie met Henry's eye. He nodded vigorously. "No, it's not," Janie said. "Give it back to me, and my friend will make it as good as new."

Sasha raised her tear-streaked face. "Really? You mean it?"

"You bet. And there's no charge either. All our dresses come with a twenty-four hour guarantee!"

When they reached Sasha's home in Rose Hill, she gave both of them a quick hug and said that it had been an evening she would remember for a long time. Janie gave Henry a quick, warm smile and agreed.

John Marquette woke the next morning with a sour stomach, a pounding head, and a mysterious ache in his jaw. He remembered bringing Sasha upstairs, but very little after that. She was gone. He prowled aimlessly around the apartment, trying to recall what had happened. Then, as he passed the big mirror on the wall opposite the waterbed, he saw the puffy lip and the fresh bruise on his cheek.

Suddenly it all came back. Braverman had had the nerve to throw a punch at him. He had made him look like a sap in front of Jenkins and Olive Oyl.

His eyes narrowed until they almost vanished. He was going to see to it that Henry Braverman regretted that punch for a long, long time!

Chapter
16

"Okay, one more time," Woody said. "When the person before you comes off the stage, there'll be a pause in the music. Start going right then, so that you and your music come in at the same time."

"What if the music doesn't come in when we do?" The question came from Jerry Bringle, Kennedy High's star squash player, who was scheduled to wear black tie and tails from Watergate Formalwear.

"Keep walking, look confident, and smile," Woody replied, trying to sound more confident than he felt. "That goes for all of you. Whatever happens, keep going, and the audience will think it's part of the show."

Woody stepped to the sidelines and glanced up at the sound booth. Peter caught his eye, gave him a nod, and said, "First model ready? Okay, and. . . ."

As the strains of a Rolling Stones song blared from the loudspeakers, he watched a senior named Mindy walk too quickly, from the bleachers to the center of the floor, turn left, and to the end of the runway he had marked with masking tape. There she stopped and waited for her cue to return.

"You're not at a bus stop," Woody called. "Hundreds of eyes are on you and your clothes. Move. Turn. Give them something to look at."

"Yeah," a male voice called from the crowd, "take off the clothes."

Over the laughter, another voice said, "No, better yet, leave them on!"

"That's enough," Woody said angrily. Poor Mindy looked ready to sink through the floor. "This is hard enough to do without a bunch of dumb jokes, so why don't you hold them until after the show."

"I see a few things I'd like to hold, huh, huh," the first voice called. That got a few whistles and some angry looks from girls who were already feeling self-conscious and unsure of themselves.

Woody easily spotted the main troublemaker: John Marquette.

He hadn't wanted to have Marquette in the show at all, but Phoebe argued that they couldn't invite stars from other sports and leave out the school's champion wrestler. He had warned her that Marquette would make trouble, and his warning was already proving to be right.

"John," he called, "can I talk to you for a minute? Okay, Mindy, thanks. You can walk off-stage now. Walk," he said more loudly as she broke into a little trot.

171

Marquette swaggered over, right across the path of the next model. "I want to talk to you, too, Webster," he said in an ominous voice.

"Whatever it is, it can wait. Changing your attitude can't," Woody said firmly. Inwardly he was quaking. Talking to Marquette was like standing in front of a truck. Everything was fine until he decided to move; then it was get out of the way or get crushed. "You're going to have to cut out the jokes and the smutty remarks. They're putting everybody on edge. Any more of it and I may have to drop you from the show."

"Listen, shrimp, I don't let clowns like you tell me what to do. I'm going to tell you what to do. Some of us are really peeved that a good friend of ours has been kept out of this Mickey Mouse production. In fact, we're so peeved that if she doesn't get put in, we might decide to take a walk. Or we might decide to stay around and make you, and your fashion show, the joke of the year."

"I don't know what you're talking about," said Woody, who knew perfectly well.

"I'm talking about Laurie Bennington, that's what. She has the best body in the junior class, and we want to see it out there on that runway in some hot outfit. Get it?"

Woody cleared his throat. "Laurie could have been in the show," he began. "We asked her. But first she wanted to pick the other models, and then she wanted to wear her own clothes, things she has at home. We had to say no."

"Yeah," Marquette growled. "Well, now you have to say yes. You've already picked all the models, right?" Woody nodded reluctantly. "Then

172

it comes down to what she wears. Who cares? Laurie's got some dynamite outfits. You've seen her. Let her wear one in the show." He didn't actually say, "or else," but it hung in the air between them.

"Er, I'll have to talk to Phoebe," Woody said nervously.

"Okay, but do it fast. This rehearsal won't get far unless we hear that Laurie's in the show."

"No!" Phoebe pushed her red hair back from her face with both hands. "Why should I bust my buttons to put together a fashion show, just to let that lying, scheming — just to let Laurie Bennington flaunt her bod? She can put her own show together — she does, just about every day, anyway!"

"Check," said Woody. "I'm with you all the way. "But. . . ."

"I knew it," Phoebe groaned. "With Laurie there's always a but around."

"But," Woody continued as if Phoebe hadn't spoken, "unless we put Laurie in, over half of our male models will quit. Or say they will."

"Why?" Phoebe wailed. "They can't *all* have the hots for her, can they?"

"Lots of reasons. Some of them are scared to go out there in front of a lot of people and are happy to have an excuse not to. Some of them think that you and I are discriminating against Laurie because we don't like her. . . ."

"Among other good reasons," Phoebe murmured.

". . . and some either want to do John

173

Marquette a favor or are scared *not* to when he asks them to."

"Hmph. Did you notice that bruise on his cheek today?"

Woody, puzzled by the question, nodded.

Phoebe smiled maliciously. "Remind me to tell you how he got it," she said. "I talked to Sasha over the weekend and got the whole story."

"Okay. But we've still got a choice to make: Laurie in the show or most of the guys out of it." Woody paused and looked at Phoebe as if he expected her to say something. When she didn't he went on. "Look, Pheebarooni, how much harm can she do? We let her walk out there in some costume, people clap, and she walks back. Period. She's happy, Marquette's happy, and we're happy because we've still got our show."

Phoebe narrowed her eyes and set her jaw. "No, we don't," she said. "If we let Laurie force us to do what she wants, it isn't our show anymore. It's hers! Next she'll make us change the order or tell us who is going to wear which outfit. She'll end up running everything, just the way she wanted to!"

Woody put his arm around Phoebe and gave her shoulder a reassuring squeeze. "Never mind, Pheeb. If you feel that strongly, we'll keep her out. Marquette and his friends can go off and do their lifts and jerks, or whatever it is they do in their free time. If we juggle the order of appearance, we can probably use most of the other guys twice. If the sizes work out."

"No, that's okay," Phoebe said with a sigh. "I was just letting off steam. There's something about

174

Laurie that makes me nervous. That's all. If we're both watching out for her schemes, we should be able to keep her from getting away with anything. Maybe all she wants is to be in the show. And maybe it wasn't fair of us to try to keep her out."

"Whoa!" Woody said. "Next thing you'll be wanting to give her your job! The reason we're letting her in is that Jolting Johnny and his friends are forcing us to. It's best for the show. Which, as everybody knows, must go on!"

In one of the curtained enclosures at the other end of the gym, Janie was checking the clothes that were going to be in the show for dangling threads and loose buttons, while Henry touched them up with an iron. She looked across when he said, "Ouch!"

He was cradling his right hand and massaging the fingers.

He grimaced. "You know, before giving me a spanking, my dad always used to say that it hurt him worse than it did me. That was when I decided not to trust anything he said. But you know what? I think that punch probably hurt me worse than it did Marquette!"

"I'm still surprised at you," Janie said. "But if anybody ever deserved to be punched, John Marquette did."

"It seemed like the kind of logic he would listen to," Henry said. "Did you see him today? I passed him in the gym a little while ago. I was afraid he'd tear my head off and dribble it down the court. But he just gave me the evil eye. In a way that worries me more."

"Yeah," Janie agreed. "He's not the type to forgive and forget. But a guy like that must make a lot of enemies. Maybe you're not very high on his list. Look at this," she added, holding up a navy blue jacket. "They must get a hundred fifty dollars or more for this blazer, and the cuff buttons are ready to fall off."

"That's why we're checking."

They worked on in silence. Then Janie said, "Sasha was thrilled when I gave her the dress this morning. She couldn't believe that you had put on a whole new sleeve. She insisted on paying ten dollars extra, and said that her story about the show will be one long rave for the Mystery Designer. I wish he would stop being a mystery."

"He's not, to you," he said.

"You've got to face it sooner or later," she insisted.

"I'll take later. The later the better. Hey, I didn't tell you! I've won a stay of execution!"

"What are you talking about?"

"My father! One of the guys in the athletics department at the college quit in the middle of everything to move out west. That means Dad will have to cover some of his classes, and help coach the swim team. And *that* means that he won't be able to come to any basketball games after all. I'm saved!" He looked at her suspiciously. "Well, why aren't you congratulating me?"

Janie refused to meet his eye. After a long silence, she said, "I don't like it. All this lying and sneaking around makes you into somebody else, somebody I don't think I like very much.

Just listen to yourself, rejoicing because your dad has to do a lot of extra work!"

Henry turned away. "It isn't my fault," he said sullenly. "If he cared at all about the real me, it might be different. But all he wants is a junior version of himself."

"Maybe he isn't as rigid as you think," Janie suggested gently. "The only way to find out is to try."

"Sure, and maybe if I jump off the Washington Monument I'll find out that I know how to fly!"

Janie felt brave enough to say, "You're only getting sarcastic because you know I'm right. You've never given your father a chance to care about the real you, because you've never let him even see the real you."

"I won't, either, if I can help it. Not until I'm old enough to go out on my own. Look, Janie," he added in a softer tone, "maybe you are right. But I can't do it, I just can't. Not won't — can't."

She put her hand on his shoulder. "All right," she said. "I didn't mean to preach. I'm no expert at getting along with parents myself."

"From what I've seen, you and your mom are getting along really well."

"That's true," Janie replied in a voice full of surprise. "She's really very nice when she isn't telling me what to do all the time. By the way, she's arranged for the twins to go to a neighbor's after school so that she can come to the show. I hope she forgets to bring the camera. If a flash goes off in my face, I'll probably trip over my own feet and ruin the effect of your gorgeous dress."

* * *

When John Marquette smiled, his cheeks almost met his eyebrows, hiding his tiny eyes completely. Those who faced him in the wrestling ring learned to fear that smile more than his scowl. It meant that he had gained an advantage and meant to use it.

He was smiling as he stepped out from behind the temporary curtain and watched the two he had been eavesdropping on walk away. Henry and Olive Oyl. What a laugh! But not nearly as big a laugh as his other discovery: Coach Braverman's son, while pretending to be a basketball star, was a secret dressmaker!

This had been quite an afternoon. He had made that clown Webster crawl, and in the process had done a big favor for luscious Laurie. She owed him now, and he never forgot a debt that someone owed him. Henry Braverman owed him, too, for that sucker punch, and now he had a surefire way to collect. The only question now was when.

Chapter
17

Coach Braverman lowered his newspaper, took another sip of his coffee, and said, "Well, son, what do you think of your chances against Millville? That forward of theirs looks pretty strong, doesn't he?"

Henry froze. These were the worst moments of his life, when his father tried to make conversation with him. The subject was always the same, sports, and he knew that sooner or later he was going to make a blunder he couldn't explain away. In self-defense, he kept his replies as short and noncommital as he could.

"It's hard to say," he said.

"Is your coach a zone defense man?"

Henry had only a vague notion of what that was, and no idea at all what the correct answer was. "Yeah, sort of," he said, staring down at his cereal bowl.

"I think we're due for more snow," Mrs.

Braverman said. "Look at that sky; doesn't that look like snow to you?"

Henry, grateful for the diversion, looked out the window. The sky was an unrelieved blanket of gray. "It sure does, Mom," he said, with such enthusiasm that anyone listening would have thought that he had been praying for snow for weeks. "That was some snow we had Friday night, wasn't it? It made me a little nervous, driving back from Georgetown in it. They hadn't gotten around to plowing the roads yet."

Mr. Braverman struck in. "A good driver doesn't need to get nervous about a little snow. It's all in your attitude."

Henry ignored this comment. "Oh, Mom, I don't think I'll be home for dinner tonight," he said.

"Why not? You haven't been here much since the holidays. Is something going on you're not telling us about?" The twinkle in her eye said that she suspected him of having a girl friend.

Henry gulped. "Oh no, it's just that some of us are planning to go out for pizza together."

"Well, remember that you have a family that likes to see your face now and then. Just so we won't forget what you look like."

"Leave the boy alone, Marian. It's important for him to go out with his buddies. Some of my finest memories are of times I spent hanging around with my teammates. Right, son?"

"Sure, Dad."

"Say, that reminds me. I had a telephone call last night from a schoolmate of yours named John Marquette. He wants to come talk to me later this

180

week. I have hopes that I can sell him on coming to Rose Hill State after he finishes high school. He'd be an asset to the football team, of course, and it sure wouldn't hurt the college's reputation to attract a state-ranked wrestler."

Under the table, Henry's right hand clenched into a fist. He didn't trust John Marquette. He wouldn't dare tell about the fight, that would mean admitting that Henry had punched him out. Marquette wasn't likely to tell anyone that embarrassing fact. But he certainly intended to do something to get back at Henry, and making an appointment with Mr. Braverman was obviously part of it.

Coach Braverman continued. "If you happen to be talking to John, you might put in a good word for our sports program at Rose Hill. These last few years we've been getting more of the wrong sort of student at the college. I've seen what that does to the morale and spirit of my players. They need to know that they have the respect and admiration of their schoolmates. What we need is more students like John Marquette. From what I can see, he's a fine athlete and the sort of student any college could be proud of."

"Marquette?" Henry blurted. "You've got to be kidding! He's a jerk! He's about the biggest jerk in the school!"

"Now just a minute, son! You shouldn't say things like that about a fellow athlete. In the first place it's bad sportsmanship, and in the second place it's disrespectful to me. I expect you to withdraw that remark and apologize."

Henry knew that the safest course was to back

down, but something wouldn't let him do it. "I won't apologize for telling the truth," he said in a rising voice. "Marquette is a vulgar bully with the manners of a pig, and the brain of a cockroach!"

" 'A vulgar bully?' " his father repeated. "That's no way to talk. What would your friends say about you in the locker room if they heard you talk like that?"

"Is that the only thing that counts?" Henry said, pushing his chair back and jumping to his feet. "What they'll say in the locker room?"

"It'll do," his father shot back. "A man's teammates get to know him better than anyone else. If they don't accept him, there's something rotten about him."

"Or something different that they don't have the brains to understand!"

"Don't you answer back to me, young man! And sit down. I haven't finished talking to you!"

"Why don't we all calm down and lower our voices," Mrs. Braverman said. "A quarrel is no way to start the day."

Neither Henry nor his father noticed.

"You know I'm right, son. Playing together, counting on each other, you find out what a fellow's worth, whether he's got the real stuff. You've seen it on the basketball team, haven't you? Come on, admit it!"

"I haven't seen anything on the basketball team!" The words came out before Henry considered their consequences. The moment he heard them, the angry blood drained from his face.

His father looked as if he couldn't decide

182

whether he was puzzled or angry. "What do you mean?" he demanded. "You've got eyes, don't you?"

There was no turning back. "I'm not on the basketball team."

"You're not?" Coach Braverman frowned in thought. "You mean you got cut from the team and were ashamed to tell me? Listen, son, it's no disgrace to —"

Henry couldn't stand the sympathy in his father's voice. "I didn't get cut," he shouted. "I never went out! I lied to you!"

The words seemed to echo forever in the silent kitchen. Finally, to fill the emptiness, Henry said, "You forced me to. You said I had to go out for some team, and I — I didn't want to. So I made it up, to keep you off my case."

His father's face reddened and seemed to swell in size. "To keep me off your case?" he roared. "Well, fellow, I'm on your case now, and I'm going to stay on it until I get some straight answers! And you can bank on that!"

His chair fell backwards as he surged to his feet and started around the breakfast table. Henry refused to retreat. When the two were practically nose to nose, Mr. Braverman barked, "What about all those times you said you were at basketball practice? What were you really doing?"

Henry had known this question was coming and he was ready for it. "I was teaching myself how to draw and how to design clothes," he said.

"To do *what*? What do you mean? What kind of clothes?"

183

"Dresses, mostly. That's what I want to do, be a designer."

"How interesting," Mrs. Braverman said brightly. "There was a designer on Johnny Carson a couple of weeks ago, a very interesting man."

"I don't care about him or Johnny Carson," the coach declared loudly. "What I care about is that my son has been sneaking around, lying to us, pretending to be something he isn't!"

"I don't have to listen to this," Henry said. "I'm already late for school. I'm getting out of here."

"Sure, run away! Act like a coward instead of staying and taking your medicine! But mark my words, I will find out what you've been up to all this time."

"Oh yeah?" Henry said. "You can start this afternoon. Student government is sponsoring a fashion show at school, with clothes from the best stores in Washington, and they're going to feature *my* designs. Not only that, in the last two weeks I've made over three hundred dollars selling dresses I created, and that's just the beginning!"

Henry picked up his books from the dining room table, grabbed his coat from the hall closet, and left the house without another word.

Chapter
18

"Even a gridiron star like Ted needs to relax sometimes, and what better way to relax than to take up the boomerang? Yes, folks, you get a snappy comeback every time!"

The audience greeted this effort of Woody's with groans and laughter.

"Ted's outfit," he continued, "courtesy of Superjock in Georgetown, includes an authentic Rugby-style shirt of extra-heavy cotton knit in teal and burgundy, canvas Rugby shorts in teal with burgundy details, and, in case of rain, matching jacket and cap in burgundy Gore-Tex. And with all that burgundy, he'll probably need somebody to help him find his way home!" When the laughter and applause died down, he added, "Phoebe, what's new on your side of the room?"

The music segued from Stevie Wonder to John Denver.

"Well, Woody," Phoebe said into the left-hand microphone, "Marcia likes to take long quiet walks along deserted country roads, and Milovan's helps her to do it in comfort and style. She's wearing a long pleated skirt in a navy and green tartan, unexpectedly topped with a snow-flake-pattern cardigan in navy and white with crimson trim. A navy and white tartan scarf wrapped around her neck adds loads of eye-catching appeal." More applause.

In the curtained area that was serving as the girls' dressing room, Janie tried to stop listening. At this rate, it would be at least twenty more minutes before her turn came. She was the very last one on the program. Phoebe had switched the order after seeing her new dress. "It's doubly fair," she had explained. "Your dress is the most exciting thing in the show, and it was designed and made by a Kennedy student. You look fantastic in it, by the way. Your friend obviously knows you really well."

Janie couldn't help blushing. Fortunately, Phoebe didn't notice, or she might have guessed the truth. She had seen Janie and Henry together more than once, and as Sasha Jenkins's best friend she had probably heard all about the fracas on Friday night.

Poor Henry! He was still wrecked by the fight with his father that morning. Janie had tried all during lunch to calm him, but she wasn't sure that he had heard her at all. She was proud of him for telling his dad the truth and was certain it was the only right thing to do. Still, part of her did wish that he had waited another day or two,

186

instead of spoiling what should have been a great day for both of them.

He was hanging around backstage somewhere. For a moment she considered going to look for him. He needed her, and the truth was, she needed him. How could she walk out there at all, without the confidence he inspired in her? But Phoebe had been very clear: Once you're in your outfit, stay in the dressing room until your turn comes. Don't spoil the effect of what you're wearing by showing it too soon, and don't upstage the other models.

Of course, Phoebe herself was doing some upstaging. As co-emcee, she was out front during the whole show, and she was wearing the dark green two-piece outfit Henry had designed for her. The effect, with her red curls cascading down over the shoulders, was stunning. Henry was also represented, more formally, by Chris, who was modeling the dress he had made for her. And when Sasha came back to interview some of the participants, Janie had been pleased to see that she was wearing her lilac dress.

If only Henry wasn't to wrapped up in his anger to see what a tribute this was to him.

"Why, hello, Janie, are *you* in the show?"

The tone of barely-disguised astonishment made Janie clench her teeth. She managed to say, "Hi, Laurie. How are you?"

Laurie was already wearing her outfit: a white mini-jumper scrawled with neon pink graffitti, over white lace tights. She had on high-heeled neon-pink ankle boots, and a neon-pink scarf held up an off-center fountain of dark hair. She looked as though she must have spent half an hour making up her eyes. The total effect was certainly striking.

"Oh, of course," Laurie continued, ignoring Janie's greeting. "Peter is one of the people running the show, isn't he? I've always said that his strong point is his loyalty to his friends."

She clearly meant that Janie had been selected only because she was a friend of Peter's. Having heard the tale of how Laurie had gotten in, Janie was tempted to laugh in her face. But the last thing she needed now was a battle with Laurie, so she gave her a meaningless smile and returned to her paperback.

Laurie, however, was not ready to give up. "What a sweet dress," she said. "Was it sewn by your little friend that all the girls are talking about? I think it's so cute for her to be trying to make dresses all on her own. I might even order some, just to give her some encouragement."

This time Janie's smile was more genuine. She could imagine the sort of outfit Henry might design to suit Laurie's personality. For a start, the sleeves would end in a set of retractable claws.

At the entrance to the dressing area there was more bustle than usual. Janie glanced over. An older woman with fluffy reddish hair had just come in carrying a clothes bag. Janie recognized her at once. She was the manager of Rezato, the boutique in Georgetown. She was the one who had yelled at Janie the day she distributed *The Red and the Gold*.

"Where shall I hang these?" she asked the girls. Janie jumped up, took the clothes bag from her, and put it on the rack at the far end of the room.

"Thank you, dear. That's the deep purple jumpsuit in a size five and the raincoat in a seven long."

"Hello, Miss Wainwright," Laurie said. "I'm Laurie Bennington. We had a nice talk the last time I was in the shop, about a possible fashion feature on my father's cable station."

"Yes, of course, dear. How are you?"

"Great!" She struck a pose. "How do you like my outfit?"

The woman ran a practiced eye over Laurie's garb and said, "Very nice, dear. Excuse me for a moment."

She walked straight over to Janie. "Excuse me, dear, but your dress — it must be one of the designs I've been hearing about."

"That's right," Janie replied anxiously.

"Tell me, who is this mysterious designer? It's hard to believe that she's a high school student."

"A friend of mine," Janie said, "who wants to stay anonymous."

"But you can speak for her. . . . Oh, I see." Miss Wainwright obviously thought that Janie herself had designed the dresses. "Well, please tell your friend to give me a call in the next few days. Tell her I've looked at her creations and I am very impressed. I'd like to explore the possibility of her creating a line exclusively for Rezato."

It was all Janie could do to keep herself from grabbing the woman and kissing her. "Thank you," she said gravely. "I'll do that."

"Please don't forget. And let me say that your dress is a triumph. It so exactly suits you."

"Thank you," Janie repeated.

Laurie had been listening to some of the conversation. Now she thrust herself forward and said, "But Miss Wainwright, what about my outfit? Isn't it too utterly now?"

"Yes, dear," the Rezato manager replied indulgently. "Of course it is. But you see, in this business we can't worry too much about being now. Now is already passé. We have to think about what will look good a year from now."

The tone of kindness made the insult even more wounding. Her face burning, Laurie rushed away. But before she left, she gave Janie a look of scorn for having witnessed her humiliation.

"Psst! Janie!"

The urgent whisper came from the other side of the curtain. She pulled back the flap and looked out. Henry was standing there chewing on his lower lip and looking very anxious. She gave him a quick hug and a kiss on the cheek. "I have the most wonderful news," she whispered.

"Tell me later. You're on in a few minutes. Did the woman from Rezato show up with a raincoat?"

"Yes, a little while ago, and you know what? She —"

"Put it on," he said, interrupting her.

"The raincoat?" she asked, bewildered.

"Uh-huh. Phoebe and I were talking, and we decided your dress will have more impact that way. You go out in the raincoat, then at the end of the runway you slip it off and make a couple of turns before walking off. Just leave the coat on the floor. Phoebe will pick it up. Got it?"

"I guess so. But —"

"Good. Go get it, let me see it on you."

She returned with the coat, which was made of a lustrous dark gray material. It buttoned only from the neck to the waist but reached almost to her ankles, like a military overcoat in a movie about Napoleon. Henry studied it critically, then nodded. "Just right." He tucked in a single lock of hair and nodded again. "Janie," he said, "you're going to knock their socks off!" The sudden grin made him look about twelve.

"Henry?" she said, as a tentative idea began to form. "The reason you didn't want anybody to know who you are was because of your dad, right?"

At the mention of his father, Henry scowled. "Right."

"But after this morning, he knows, doesn't he? Why shouldn't other people know? I want to see you get the credit you deserve."

His face revealed conflict, as if he had become too used to anonymity to give it up.

"Janie?" the stage manager called. "You're next!"

She hurriedly put her arms around Henry's neck, not caring who saw. "Watch me," she whispered. "And listen. Wish me luck."

"Luck," he whispered back, and gave her a brief, tender kiss.

"Henry," she scolded, "don't wrinkle my dress."

"Now, ladies and gentlemen," Phoebe's voice

boomed over the opening chords of a Posers song, "to cap our show, Janie is on her way to a grand embassy reception, but she's ready for any weather. Her coat, in nylon ciré, is the talk of Milan, and can be found in the Washington area only at Rezato in Georgetown."

Janie walked steadily, slowly, down the marked runway, holding her head as high as a queen. *Henry, this is for you*, she thought. The applause for the coat died away, but one person applauded a few seconds longer. She glanced over and exchanged a fleeting smile with her clapping mom. For a moment, Janie thought her father also had come to see the show. Then she realized that the man standing next to her mom, arms folded across his chest, was Henry's father! He had come to the show after all that had happened!

At the end of the runway, Janie unbuttoned the coat as Phoebe said, "Janie's dress was designed for her by a student here at Kennedy High School whose identity is a secret." The smooth lining of the sleeves slipped easily down her arms, revealing the asymetrical gray dress, the bare left shoulder, and the slashing stripe of bright raspberry. As the applause swelled, Janie turned slowly to the left, raised her arms to shoulder height, and turned back to the right.

This was the moment when she was supposed to turn around and walk back up the runway. Instead, she stepped over the masking tape border and walked over to the microphone. A startled Phoebe backed away.

"Ladies and gentlemen," Janie said in a voice that trembled, "I'd like to make an announcement.

192

No, two announcements." She looked across the open space straight at Henry's father. "First, the student who designed my dress is an incredibly talented person, and a very good friend of mine —"

That got a warm, knowing laugh from the audience.

"— named Henry Braverman, Junior. He's hiding out backstage, but I hope he can hear what I'm saying."

They clapped for that, more loudly than they had for the dress.

"And my second announcement . . . and this will come as a surprise to Henry . . . is that Rezato will soon feature an exclusive line of his designs."

The clapping turned to cheers for the talent and success of a fellow student. Before the applause had died, Janie was backstage, in Henry's arms.

"Janie, how could you?" he demanded fondly. "I nearly died when I heard your voice come over the loudspeaker!"

"I had to," she laughed breathlessly. "I couldn't let the show end without everybody knowing the name of the person who designed the best dresses in the show, could I?" She gave him another kiss, then pulled back to confess, "I was so scared, walking over and taking the mike! I just knew that I was going to open my mouth and nothing would come out!"

"Oh, it came out all right! But what was that stuff about Rezato?"

"I tried to tell you. The manager of Rezato saw all your dresses today and thought they were fantastic, and she asked me to tell you to talk to her about designing an exclusive line of dresses for her shop!"

His jaw dropped. "You mean you were serious? I thought you were making some off-the-wall joke. Do you realize what this means?"

She grabbed his neck, pulled his head down, and kissed him on the nose. "Of course I do," she said proudly. "It means that you're already starting to have the success you deserve! Are you going to forget your old friends, now that you're a famous designer?"

He tightened his arms and let a long kiss answer her question. "Janie, I love you," he said. "Everything is turning out perfectly, and it's all because of you. I've never been so happy. Even the fight with my father seems unimportant compared to this."

"Henry, I love you, too," Janie said, still holding him tight. "I feel like a brand-new person because of you —"

He silenced her with another kiss. Then they had to separate, to deal with all the people who wanted to congratulate them.

Sasha was the first. "You're so clever, Janie Barstow," she said with a hug, "telling me your friend might fix my dress when he was right there in the front seat. Do you think he'd mind if I kissed him? I love my dress so much."

"I'm sure he wouldn't," Janie said, laughing. "But I might."

After a few minutes, Janie disengaged herself and went out front. Her mom was still there, and so was Henry's father. She went over to them.

"Janie, you were lovely, and your dress is

194

terrific," Mrs. Barstow exclaimed. "I had to pinch myself to make sure I wasn't dreaming! And what do you think? This gentleman I've been chatting with during the show actually turns out to be Henry's father!"

"I know," Janie said gravely. "I'm glad you came, Mr. Braverman."

"So am I, young lady. Well, it was nice to meet you both. I'd better —"

"Mr. Braverman," Janie said, "Henry is back-stage. Would you like to say hello?"

He hesitated.

"I think Henry would be glad to see you," she added, hoping she was right.

"Well, yes, I'd like that." He followed her across the gym floor and through the curtains. Henry was talking to Woody and Phoebe, but he looked up and saw his father. He became very still.

Coach Braverman was equally quiet. The moment stretched out. Then the older man cleared his throat, put out his hand, and strode across the distance that divided him from his son.

"Henry, I want to congratulate you," he said, shaking his hand and clapping him on the shoulder. "Today was a real triumph for you. I'm proud of you."

"Thanks, Dad. I —" With a sudden impulsive movement, he put his arms around his father. After an almost unnoticeable hesitation, his father returned the embrace.

Henry met Janie's gaze over his father's shoulder. His glistening eyes told her everything he wanted to say and she wanted to hear.

* * *

John Marquette dropped the camouflage outfit on the floor by the clothes rack, scowled at himself in the mirror, and straightened his letter jacket. He sauntered out of the dressing room just in time to see Henry the Wimp putting his arms around some man. He had his nerve, acting like that right in front of everybody. John was ready to make a loud, gross joke when the man turned in his direction, and he recognized Coach Braverman. His scowl deepened. So Henry and his old man were on good terms again, were they? That was a shame. He turned and left the gym. On the front steps, two freshmen scurried out of his path, bringing a smile back to his lips.

Sasha noticed Marquette leave and breathed easier. She had been afraid that he would spoil the afternoon by picking a fight with Henry. How strange that Henry turned out to be the Masked Designer! He and Janie were still talking to Henry's father and Janie's mother. Both of them looked very confident and mature, and very much in love. Was that what had transformed Janie from the timid girl who had crept into the newspaper office a couple of months before? Sasha found it hard to believe that this was the same person.

At the thought of the newspaper, Sasha became tired. Everything had been such a hassle lately that the thrill had gone out of her work. Oh, she knew she'd get it back — she loved journalism too much not to — but she was beginning to feel that by spending so much time on the paper she was missing other important things. A lump came to her throat as she watched Janie and Henry walk away arm in arm, but she smiled and told herself that a better time was coming for her, too. She hoped it would come soon.

Coming Soon...
Couples #5
MOVING TOO FAST

Sasha stepped back as she turned around, bumping smack into a boy who stood behind her, also admiring Jefferson's portrait. "Oh excuse me!" she exclaimed.

"Excuse *me!* If anything, it's my fault. I — I should have gotten out of the way," the boy said, a trace of a southern lilt in his deep voice.

Sasha took a good look at him. His strong face and finely chiseled features were framed by short, straight dark hair. His eyes were green, deep-set, and fringed with long black lashes. Her gaze locked with his, and everything else in the room seemed to melt away. All that existed for Sasha at that moment was the boy, her nearness to him, and the pounding of her heart.

She tried to catch her breath, moving a few steps back. She took in the boy's broad shoulders, his muscular frame clad in a gray sweat shirt and jeans. She felt him drinking in her appearance, too.

The spell was shattered when two younger boys burst into the room, each grabbing one of his arms. "Hey, dingdong, are you gonna stand here all day?" the bigger of the two pestered. They pulled him toward the next room.

Sasha remained rooted to the spot. Her pulse raced and her cheeks felt flushed. Her fingers trembled. What was happening to her? If ever there was such a thing as love at first sight, this was it!

CHEERLEADERS™

Join the Team!

They're talented. They're fabulous-looking. They're winners! And they've got what you want! Don't miss any of these exciting CHEERLEADERS books!

Watch for these titles! $2.25 each

☐ QI 33402-6 **Trying Out** *Caroline B. Cooney*
☐ QI 33403-4 **Getting Even** *Christopher Pike*
☐ QI 33404-2 **Rumors** *Caroline B. Cooney*
☐ QI 33405-0 **Feuding** *Lisa Norby*
☐ QI 33406-9 **All the Way** *Caroline B. Cooney*
☐ QI 33407-7 **Splitting** *Jennifer Sarasin*
